"Come with ... ..., ..., ..."

"There's no cowboy named K.C. There's no Countess. There's only Kent Coleman Landover, and he most definitely isn't in love with a cleaning lady. You don't remember now, but one day, you will."

He grasped her arms. "There is a lot I don't remember. I don't remember how I made all this money or why I built a big white box of a house or why I spent my days behind a desk in a room where the windows don't open. They tell me I did all of that, and at this point, I've got to believe them, because I don't remember anything... except for one thing."

He reached for a stray strand of her hair, lifting it gently. "I remember you, Anna. You and me."

Dear Reader,

Spring is coming with all its wonderful scents and colors, and here at Harlequin American Romance we've got a wonderful bouquet of romances to please your every whim!

Few women can refuse a good bargain, but what about a sexy rancher who needs a little help around the house? Wait till you hear the deal Megan Ford offers Rick Astin in Judy Christenberry's *The Great Texas Wedding Bargain*, the continuation of her beloved miniseries TOTS FOR TEXANS!

Spring is a time for new life, and no one blossoms more beautifully than a woman who's WITH CHILD.... In *That's Our Baby!*, the first book in this heartwarming new series, Pamela Browning travels to glorious Alaska to tell the story of an expectant mother and the secret father of her child.

Then we have two eligible bachelors whose fancies turn not lightly, but rather unexpectedly, to thoughts of love. Don't miss *The Cowboy and the Countess*, Darlene Scalera's tender story about a millionaire who has no time for love until a bump on the head brings his childhood sweetheart back into his life. And in Rita Herron's *His-and-Hers Twins*, single dad Zeke Blalock is showered with wife candidates when his little girls advertise for a mother...but only one special woman will do!

So this March, don't forget to stop and smell the roses— and enjoy all four of our wonderful Harlequin American Romance titles!

Happy reading!

Melissa Jeglinski
Associate Senior Editor

The Cowboy and the Countess

DARLENE SCALERA

HARLEQUIN®

TORONTO • NEW YORK • LONDON
AMSTERDAM • PARIS • SYDNEY • HAMBURG
STOCKHOLM • ATHENS • TOKYO • MILAN • MADRID
PRAGUE • WARSAW • BUDAPEST • AUCKLAND

To my children, J.J. and Ariana. You are my heart.

Acknowledgment: Special thanks to Gail Fiorini-Jenner, teacher, writer and cattle rancher, for her generosity and patience with a tenderfoot.

ISBN 0-373-16819-5

THE COWBOY AND THE COUNTESS

Copyright © 2000 by Darlene Scalera.

Printed in U.S.A.

ABOUT THE AUTHOR

Darlene Scalera is a native New Yorker who grad-
uated magna cum laude from Syracuse University
with a degree in public communications. She worked
in a variety of fields, including telecommunications
and public relations, before devoting herself full-time
to romance fiction writing. She was instrumental in
forming the Saratoga, New York, chapter of Romance
Writers of America and is a frequent speaker on
romance writing at local schools, libraries, writing
groups and women's organizations. She currently
lives happily ever after in upstate New York with her
husband, Jim, and their two children, J.J. and
Ariana. You can write to Darlene at P.O. Box 217,
Niverville, NY 12130.

Books by Darlene Scalera

HARLEQUIN AMERICAN ROMANCE
762—A MAN FOR MEGAN
807—MAN IN A MILLION
819—THE COWBOY AND THE COUNTESS

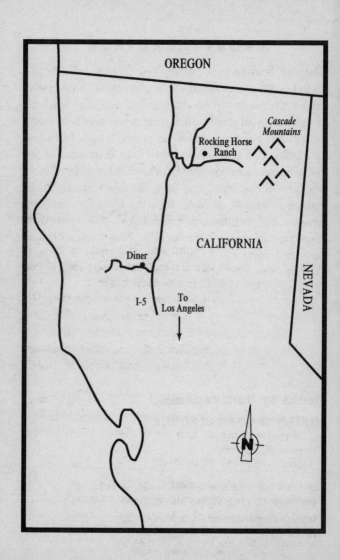

Chapter One

"If he's a cowboy, then I'm a kielbasa," the man declared.

"Kielbasa." The word felt full, fun on K.C.'s tongue, and he smiled. To the man at the foot of his bed, he asked, "You're a foreigner, then?"

The man looked down the length of the bed. He was squat and fierce. His cheeks were red as if burned by a fast razor, and he spoke in spasms broken by greedy gulps of air. But when K.C. looked him in the eyes, he felt the familiarity of an old friend. He liked this man.

The man attempted a smile. The effort only diminished some of the slack in his razor-scraped cheeks. "I'm not a foreigner, and you're not a cowboy. Your name is Kent—"

"Landover."

"You know your name?" Now the man smiled, his neck bulging above his shirt collar. A red dot rose on the expanded flesh, a lone pimple beheaded. Another victim of the wounding razor.

"Yessir, I know my own name."

The man glanced at the white-coated trio behind him. He looked back at K.C., his eyes rich velvet triumph.

"But everyone calls me K.C."

The man's eyes dulled.

"Now I understand your confusion about the cowboyin'. Tethered to this bed, trussed up in this getup—" K.C. plucked at the faded front of the gown "—I hardly look like a man who can brand several hundred calves in a day and birth a few more in the night, if need be. But believe me, in here—" he flattened a palm across his chest "—there beats the heart of one of the last true wranglers."

The man looked at him, his expression glazed. He muttered several profanities. "Listen to me, you're no cowboy. You're the founder, the CEO of Landover Technology. Generation X's golden boy. The digital era's David. The youngest head honcho of a company ever to earn a Fortune 500 ranking. Cowboy?" The man's fleshy cheeks jiggled as he spoke. "Cowboy?"

One of the white-coated trio stepped forward and touched the fat-faced man's elbow.

The man turned. "You know he's Kent Landover." His voice ballooned; his body seemed to expand. He looked at the other two men in white. "You know he's Kent Landover."

The white coats were doctors, K.C. decided. The one now murmuring to the florid man had fine lines around the mouth and eyes that spoke of too many deaths and too few miracles. He held a chart in one hand and, with the other, steered the sputtering man toward the hall.

"I'm telling you, the man lying there is the same man named 1994 Man of the Year by *PC Magazine*. CEO of the Year by *Financial World* in 1996. We land this deal with Sushima Components, and that man in there will be on the cover and in the headlines of every business publication in the world. Three-fourths of the civilized world knows he's Kent Landover. Everyone…" The man halted at the door. His flushed face turned to K.C. Their gazes caught and held. "Everyone except him."

The doctor ushered the man into the hallway.

"Is he going to be okay?" K.C. asked.

One of the other doctors looked up from the bag of yellow fluid attached by a slim hose to K.C.'s arm. He smiled with already-perfected reassurance. "He'll be fine. You rest now. We'll be right back."

The doctors left, closing the door halfway. K.C. looked out the wide room window, seeing a slice of gauzy sky wedged between too many buildings. He heard the spurt and crackle of the short man's voice outside the door. That's what comes from living too close to concrete for too long, he thought.

He laid his head back against the propped pillow and closed his eyes. He saw the mountains in the bleached light of a high noon sun. He missed home. He missed Anna.

The door swung open. The man, his neck no longer inflated and now almost too thin for his large jaw, came back into the room. He smiled at K.C., but his features kept a nauseous cast.

Behind the man came a woman, her head held erect, her beauty carried like a brocaded mantle. She smiled full, colored lips at him. He nodded, courteous, curious. She was handsome, and he was intrigued but not drawn. Her beauty was too hallowed. Where was Anna?

The woman came to his bedside, her smile serene. She leaned over and touched her smooth cheek to his forehead. His brow furrowed against her glassy flesh. His skin felt tender, bruised.

"Oh, my darling." It was between a song and a sigh. The sweep of the woman's hair fell in a dark curve, curtaining K.C.'s vision so he only saw the lower half of the short man's face. The man's lips were pursed, triangling his jaw.

The woman straightened. The white-coated chorus of doctors had returned and was watching. The woman's hand lay against his cheek. "You remember me, don't you, darling?"

He looked up into bottle-green eyes, their whites iridescent with expectation. "Are you a friend of Anna's?"

The woman's touch tensed against his face. Her eyes deepened to emerald. With a slow, elegant twist of her neck, she turned to the short man at the end of the bed. "Who's Anna?"

The man shrugged. "All he told me was he's a cowboy named K.C."

The woman's head swiveled. She looked down at him. "K.C.?"

"Yes?"

Her hand made small strokes against his cheek. She was gimlet-eyed. Her teeth were tiny and glistening. "Who's Anna?"

"The woman I love."

Her hand stilled. He watched the muscles in her slim throat ripple.

"The woman you love?"

He nodded. "I'm going to marry her...if she'll have me."

The woman's smile came back less full. Her hand stroked his cheek once. "Why would she say no to you?"

"She's a countess."

"A countess?" There was a quiver in her well-modulated tone.

"And I'm an ol' cowpuncher."

"An ol' cowpuncher named K.C.," the woman repeated. She stared at him. Her smile spread soft, indulgent.

He nodded.

"Your name isn't Kent Landover?"

"In fact, ma'am, it is."

"It is?" The woman threw a glance at the man at the end of the bed.

"That's my given name—Kent Coleman Landover." He winked at the woman, pleased she looked less upset, almost happy. "K.C., for short."

The woman's smile vanished. She straightened.

"He's only been awake for a brief time," advised the doctor holding the chart. "Any family?"

"His parents divorced when Kent was in high school. Father passed away about five years ago—heart attack," the short man said.

"His mother is on her third or fourth marriage. I've lost count. She lives somewhere abroad—Denmark, Sweden, Norway," the woman said. "One of those Scandinavian countries. She sends fabulous Icelandic sweaters at Christmas."

"No brothers or sisters?"

The man and woman both shook their heads. "Only child," the woman said.

"I knew three boys grew up on the Ponderosa Ranch in Nevada. One father, three different mothers." K.C. rolled his eyes. The others stared at him.

He sat up. There was soreness when he moved, as if he'd sat too long in a cheap saddle. "I realize I must have been off my feed, doc, but I'm feeling spry now and ready to move on."

From the corner of his eye K.C. saw the woman mouthing "off my feed."

"When do you think I can move 'em up and head 'em out?"

"Move 'em up and head 'em out," the woman's lips formed.

The doctor came to the side of the bed. "How many fingers am I holding up, Kent?"

"Call me K.C. Everyone does."

The doctor nodded. "Okay. How many fingers am I holding up, K.C.?"

K.C. smiled. "Three."

The doctor touched his forehead. "Any headaches, dizziness, nausea?"

He shook his head.

The doctor pulled down the lower lid of his right eye, then his left. "Any double vision?"

"Nope. I'm ready to saddle up and be on my way."

The doctor laid his fingertips against the inside of K.C.'s wrist. "Where would you be heading?"

K.C. looked to the window and the smog-shrouded cityscape. "I'm here to find Anna."

"She lives here in L.A.?" The doctor lifted K.C.'s arm, bent it up and down at the elbow.

K.C. nodded. "Somewhere in one of those big mansions. Bel Air or Brentwood or the Hills. She's a countess."

"So you mentioned," the doctor said. "And you're here to find her?"

K.C. nodded once more.

"To ask her to marry you?"

K.C. looked around the room, at the strange faces he didn't know. Still, he could see what they were thinking. "You all think I couldn't drive nails in a snowbank, don't you?"

Blank faces looked at him.

"It's okay if you think the fodder isn't full in the silo. It's nothing I haven't thought of myself. I mean, why would someone who has everything—fine looks, intelligence, wealth, breeding, not to mention the pick of the crop—marry someone the likes of me? You're right. I'm crazy. Crazy in love with Anna. And crazy people do crazy things. So here I am, in La-La Land, to find her, to ask her to be my wife...and make me the happiest guy alive."

The woman moved back from the bed.

"I know this might not make much sense to you all—"

A choking sound came from the woman.

"But if you'll unhook me here—" he nodded toward the tube attached to his arm "—and pronounce me fine and dandy, I'll thank you for your fine care and hospitality and be on my way." He started to shift his weight off the bed.

The doctor laid a hand on his arm. "K.C., do you remember having an auto accident this morning?"

He looked at the doctor, then up at the circle of faces again. He leaned back, smiling with relief. "Is that why you all look so worried? Here I am, spouting away like a hot spring." He started to sit up once more. "Again, I'll thank you for your concern and care, but besides feeling as if a bronc got the better of me, I'm fine." He pushed back the sheet.

Again the doctor's hand pressed on his forearm. "K.C.—"

"Kent. Kent. His name is Kent." The woman's voice split the air.

K.C. looked at her anguished face. "Ma'am, I don't mean to—"

"I'm not your 'ma'am.' Good God." She came to the bed, grasped his hands. "I'm your fiancé."

He pulled back from her imploring gaze. "Ma'am, I'm sorry, but—"

"Kent," the doctor interceded, "this morning you lost control of your vehicle and ended up in an embankment off I-5. Fortunately, your air bag engaged, and you suffered a few bruises and a concussion. However, a blow to the head often results in a loss of memory, a blocking out of critical personal information."

"What're you saying, Doc?"

"You've got amnesia."

"Amnesia?"

"Most cases last only a few days or, at the most, a few weeks. The rate of recovery is often quite amazing during the first six months after the head trauma. Often the brain just needs time to recover from the impact. Impairments could begin to disappear within days. I'd like to schedule a few more tests, but preliminary indications suggest you can expect a full recovery."

K.C. looked up at the white marble woman, the full-faced short man. He looked back at the doctor. "No one else was hurt, were they?"

"No." The doctor allayed his fear. "According to the report, you were following too close behind a bus and when it braked to take the ramp, you steered right to avoid hitting it, lost control and went over the side."

"You rolled the Range Rover good a few times," the short man noted.

K.C. looked at him, studying him. "You're...?"

"I'm your business partner, Leon Skow."

"Business partner?"

Leon chuckled, his soft cheeks shaking. "We're not exactly even-Steven, but I've been with you since you started beefing up surplus PCs and selling them from your dorm room."

"And I'm your fiancé, darling," the woman said.

He looked her way.

"Hilary Fairchild." She brushed a hand across his arm. "Don't worry. I'll take care of you, and we'll get you better in no time. After all, the wedding is less than a month away."

K.C. studied the woman's beautiful face. He saw a stranger. He looked to the man. Nothing.

Business partner, fiancé, beefed-up PCs, wedding?

"I'm sorry, but there's been a mistake. You must have me confused with another Kent Landover."

The man chuckled again. "Believe me, there's only one Kent Landover."

K.C. looked to the doctor for an explanation. The doctor watched him, said nothing.

K.C. said, "Where's Anna?"

The doctor looked at the short man, the beautiful woman.

"Darling." The woman stroked his hair, but her voice was sharp. "There's no Anna."

K.C. pulled away from her touch. He grasped the doctor's arm. "What's happened to Anna?"

The doctor looked down at the hand too tight on his wrist. "Was Anna in the Range Rover with you at the time of the accident?"

"No, she was on the bus."

"On the bus?" Hilary questioned.

"She was wearing her crown."

"Wearing her—"

He didn't hear the rest. Instead, he saw Anna as he'd seen her then. First it'd been a glimpse, so fast he wasn't sure. He'd accelerated. She'd come back into focus. The tilted tiara, the wide-set eyes, the crooked grin that made him feel good just looking at it.

How long had it been since he'd last seen her? A lifetime.

Lying there in the hospital bed, he remembered— he'd been driving on the freeway, and he'd seen Anna bigger than life on a passing bus. He'd followed the bus, memory welling into emotion. Happiness, for a few short seconds, was his once more. His life contracted to a square no larger than the narrow panel of a bus's backside. He'd seen the lights come on beneath the square, warming to red, guiding him like a beacon in a storm.

Then there'd been nothing…darkness deepening, becoming complete. Yet he hadn't been afraid. There was peace, a long, deep sigh such as he might have imagined. There was silence all around. Nothing except for his own cry, his own call.

Don't leave me, Anna.

"I saw Anna," he told the faces curved above him.

"When did you see her?" the doctor asked.

"Right before the accident."

"You remember this?"

He nodded.

"Do you remember anything else?"

"No."

The doctor glanced at the others. "Nothing?"

K.C. laid his head back against the pillows. He closed his eyes.

"I remember only Anna."

HE MUST HAVE SLEPT, because when he woke it was dark, and he was alone except for the sounds of the hospital coming from the hall. The tube that had led into his arm had been removed. An untouched tray of green Jell-O, ginger ale and a covered plastic coffee cup sat on the thin table beside his bed. He sat up slowly. He was stiffer than the day after the Laramie River Rodeo when Big, Bad Blue had bucked him high, and he'd landed low.

He slid his legs over the side of the bed and stood, then sat down as a wave of dizziness curled his knees.

"Shoot." He shook his head to clear it, scolded himself with a rueful smile. "That's what you get for taking off your boots for too long."

He made his way to the bathroom. The face that stared back at him would've been more familiar with a Stetson pulled low along the brow. He had a purplish bruise on his right cheek tender to the touch, dark circles under his eyes and a swollen shape to his brow. His blond curly hair had been cut much too short. He wondered when that had happened. Had it been necessary to treat his head injury? Didn't matter, he thought, stepping back from the mirror and going to the bed. Soon enough it'd grow back. The important part was he was alive and in L.A., and so was Anna.

He sat on the edge of the bed, poured a glass of water from the plastic pitcher on the table and took a sip. He grimaced. City water. How did Anna stand it here?

He set the cup down and pushed the table away. Leaning back on the pillows, he looked at the lights of the city, thinking. People had been here earlier—nodding doctors, a pug dog of a man, a T-bone of a woman. They'd confused him with another Kent Landover who owned some big company and was engaged to marry the lady. He stretched and folded his arms behind his head, wincing as his muscles protested. He hoped they got everything straightened out, because he didn't intend to lie around here as useless as a .22 shell in a 12-gauge shotgun. He had plans.

Wide awake, he looked around the room. He could take a walk down the hall, but then one of those nurses would be in here, prodding and poking him again. There was only one lady he wanted prodding and poking him, and tomorrow he was going to find her and pledge her his heart.

His gaze landed on the small television set angled above him. He picked up the remote control on the nightstand and pressed On, muting it as the television came to life. He didn't want to alert the nurses. He flipped through the channels, stopping at an old John Wayne movie—*Red River,* one of his favorites. He'd seen it well over a hundred times. He leaned back against the pillows, smiling as he mouthed the dialogue.

The film broke for commercials. He was stretched out and smiling. He had John Wayne tonight. Tomorrow he'd have Anna. He was a happy man.

An ad came on for A Little Bit of Seoul on Olympic Boulevard—the best in Korean barbecue. The next commercial promised you could learn to sell real estate in your spare time. Then a woman was on the screen, tap-dancing, singing. She moved her head. The light caught the gems in her crown.

K.C. sat upright. He rose, and on his knees, crossed the bed until he was below the television set. His hand reached up slowly, shaking, as if to touch a dream. He placed it full-palm on the screen. The crowned woman did a high kick.

"Anna," he whispered.

"ANNA," MAUREEN DELANEY cried as her daughter came in the back door. Breathing heavily, Anna stopped in the doorway. Maureen took a step back.

Ronnie, sitting behind the faux walnut desk, clapped her hands to rouged cheeks. "Chickie-boom-boom, was there a rumble at Sushi Boy?"

Ignoring them both, Anna moved to the middle of the room and was about to collapse into one of the chairs angled before Ronnie's desk.

"No!" her mother cried.

Anna poised midcrouch.

"Not the crushed velour."

"Oh, doll." Ronnie's hand fanned the air. "I'm penciling you in for a steam cleaning at eleven."

Striking a wide stance, Anna exhaled a breath of exasperation. Her bangs lifted, and the wisps of hairs fallen from her hasty topknot stirred.

"Come on." Now Ronnie's wave expressed impatience. "Spill the beans. Oops! That's just a figure of speech, doll face."

She and Anna's mother burst into laughter.

Anna's lips drew together. "Mrs. Lindsay stopped me during my morning run."

"Uh-oh." Ronnie rolled her eyes.

"*Child, the boy who walks my babies couldn't make it this morning,*" Anna uttered in falsetto. "*Since you're already in the midst of your morning constitutional, couldn't the puppies keep you company?*"

Ronnie, her face cradled between her palms, said, "And?"

"And? The 'puppies' are two full-grown greyhounds with legs longer than Michael Jordan's."

"Do tell?" Ronnie's eyebrows did a Groucho Marx dance.

"It would've been easier to ride one of them."

"Bareback?"

"The 'puppies' caught sight of a stray Siamese nosing around the garbage cans out back of Phil's Fine Fish Fry, and…" Anna looked down at her oversize fuchsia T-shirt and favorite striped bike shorts. They were flecked with moist green bits she prayed were relish. A glob of white creamy stuff clung to the hem of her shirt. *Please let that be mayonnaise,* she prayed, staring at the shivering form.

"Go no further. We get the picture...." Ronnie eyed her. "In glorious detail. Now go upstairs and take a shower in tomato juice or something. We're the Clean Queens, not the Grunge Girls. Any minute now, someone is going to walk through that door, and what's the first thing he sees? You prancing around the place, smelling like last Friday's flounder special."

The phone rang. Ronnie whooped. "Business is booming!" She waved her hand once more, dismissing Anna, then picked up the phone. "Clean Queens. We'll give your castle the royal treatment, and you won't have to ransom the family jewels to pay for it."

"She loves saying that, doesn't she?" Anna said to her mother as she crossed the reception area. To the left was another room with a folding table, metal chairs and easel. Anna would be training several new girls in there this morning while her mother interviewed other applicants in the opposite office. It looked as if Clean Queens would survive its first month of operation.

"Are you sure you're all right, sweetheart?" her mother asked.

Anna nodded. "As soon as I shower and change."

"Go on upstairs. Take a bubble bath," her mother told her. "You've been working too hard. If you're not here in the office, you're cleaning with the afternoon and night crews."

"How else am I going to make you a rich old woman?"

Her mother smiled. "Make sure you have some breakfast. You're getting too skinny. The scones are still warm on top of the oven. We'll be fine down here. The schedule's all set, and so far, none of the girls have called in." She crossed her fingers.

Anna stopped at the doorway that connected the offices to the apartment upstairs. "So, is business booming?"

Her mother looked up from the schedule book. "Ronnie and her theatrics aside, let's just say we're building…one dust bunny at a time. But you know those TV commercials you did?"

"Yeah?"

"They've brought in three calls."

"They only started airing two nights ago." Anna gave the thumbs-up sign.

Her mother blew her a kiss. "I'll hug you later, sweetheart, when you don't smell like Charlie the Tuna."

Anna started toward the stairs, smiling. Her mother had invested everything she could in opening her own commercial and residential cleaning business. It was a huge risk, but it had always been her mother's dream. Anna wanted to see it come true, and would do anything to see that it did—from insisting her mother borrow the money Anna had been saving toward a down payment on a house to dressing up like a cross between a bag lady and a Las Vegas chorus girl, donning a rhinestone crown, grabbing a feather-duster scepter and pirouetting across a dusty sound-stage, singing the praises of the Clean Queens.

She was at the stairs when she heard the front door chimes, announcing a newcomer. Another customer, she hoped.

"Well, hello, sailor," she heard Ronnie say. "Can I help you?"

She was at the first step when she heard a voice say, "Is Anna here?"

She stopped, a wash of heat drowning her. Everything stopped. Time reversed. Dimensions narrowed. There was nothing but that voice. A voice from her dreams.

"Who-o-o-m-m-m shall I say is calling?" Ronnie would be eyeing the man, giving him a good once-over.

"Kent? Kent Landover? Is that you?"

"Ma'am?"

"It is you—little Kent Landover. You don't remember me? Of course you don't remember me. The last time you saw me you were no more than knee-high. I'm Anna's mother, Maureen...Maureen Delaney."

"Anna's mother?" First it was a question. "Anna's mother!" Now it was glee.

"Little Kent Landover." Her mother would be shaking her head in amazement. "Look at you now, all tall and handsome and grown-up."

"Ma'am, it's an honor."

"Oh, honey, no need to stand on formality. You

always were such a serious little thing. Come on over here and give an old lady a hug.''

Anna heard Ronnie laugh. ''Yeah, sure, little Kent Landover. One of the most eligible men in America— until recently. I keep my list up-to-date, honey. Little Kent Landover waltzes into the Clean Queens, simple as you please and—''

''Oh, I'm not that Kent Landover,'' the man said.

Anna gripped the stair rail, her knuckles arranged in a white row.

''No? Which Kent Landover would you be?'' Anna heard the upward sail of Ronnie's voice and knew the large woman was standing up now, erecting a barrier. ''The poor-as-a-church-mouse illegitimate twin?''

''I'm K.C.''

Anna sank down to the bottom step. Her hand, a bony relief, clung to the rail.

''My name is Kent Landover—''

''Uh-huh.'' Anna heard the guard in Ronnie's voice. She'd be circling the corner of the desk, bringing her substantial bulk closer to the stranger.

''But I'm not that fella who owns some company out here in California.''

''No?'' Ronnie had her weapons drawn and cocked.

''No, ma'am. There seems to be some confusion about that other fella and me. I'm nothing so grand. I do a little cowboyin'—''

''Cowboyin'?'' The word, uttered in Ronnie's south Bronx accent, seemed to bounce off the ceiling and around the room.

On the step, Anna sat, listening. She felt the smile soft on her face, the tears soft on her skin.

"Okay, K. C. Cowboy, what brings you to the Clean Queens?" Ronnie's accent was more pronounced, her voice wary.

It was quiet, the moment before a storm. The breath holds. Wind stills. Birds go mute. Animals raise their heads, look with wonder. Anna's head rose now, too, turned toward the doorway and the man beyond.

"I've come..." The voice paused, then came back stronger, clearer. "I've come to ask Anna to be my bride."

Chapter Two

"What?" Ronnie exploded. The gale of voice filled the room and reached to where Anna sat. She didn't react. Shock had already stilled her.

"Ronnie." It was her mother's steady voice. "Perhaps our guest would like a cup of coffee or tea?"

"Sure. With one or two lumps of reality?"

"Ronnie." The calm was still there, but warning had been added.

Anna heard the man's voice again. "I understand you being upset and all, Miss Ronnie—"

It was different, deeper than the voice of Anna's childhood. It was the song of one girl's every fantasy.

She heard Ronnie's heavy tread. "Don't you 'Miss Ronnie' me, buster." She'd be shaking her finger in his face now. "Don't let my delicate demeanor fool you. Do you remember 'The Bam Bam Bomber' who led the Rocking Rollers all the way to the nationals in '79?"

Oh no, Anna thought. That remark always prefaced trouble. *Mama*, she prayed, *break it up before Ronnie goes for a choke slam.*

"No, ma'am, I can't say that I do, but I do understand your reservations regarding Anna and me."

"You better, buddy." There was the even, full thud of steps. Ronnie was stalking now.

"I could never be good enough for her."

"Damn straight."

"Her being a countess and all..."

Anna's hand rose to her open mouth.

"But I love her."

Anna closed her eyes.

"Are you trying to make fools of us, boy?"

"Ronnie, let go of his neck. Sit down," Anna's mother ordered. "Kent, you too, child, please have a seat. Let me fix you a nice cup of tea."

"Lace it with lithium," Ronnie suggested.

"Ronnie." Her mother's voice sharpened. Then it was soft again. "Kent, I'm going to make us some tea, and there's some scones baked fresh this morning. Do you remember my scones, Kent?"

"No, ma'am, I'm sorry to say I don't, but I've had a little trouble remembering some things lately."

"Don't give it no nevermind. It was a long time ago you last tasted my scones. Ronnie?" Her tone was firm again. "I'll only be a minute. I'll expect everything to run smoothly in my absence."

"Yeah, sure," Ronnie said. "Leave me to entertain lunatic."

There was a pause, then Ronnie said, "Cowboy, I'm not sure this town is big enough for the both of us."

Anna's mother came to the doorway, saw her

daughter sitting on the staircase step. She closed the door and sat down beside her.

"You heard?" Her voice was a balm.

Anna nodded. She didn't know what to say, what to think.

Her mother nudged her with her elbow. "Countess." One corner of her mouth tipped up into a grin.

Anna smiled even as the tears began to slip down her face again.

"Oh, darling girl." Her mother slid her arms around her. "You love him, don't you?"

"Don't be ridiculous," Anna whispered into the soft cotton of her mother's shirt.

"And he loves you."

Anna lifted her head. She saw the far-off look fill her mother's eyes and knew she'd already lost the fight. Still she had to say, "That's equally ridiculous."

"You fell in love with him when you were young, and you've loved him all this time."

"No," she protested. She laid her head on the wide square of her mother's shoulder. "We were children."

"As were your father and I," her mother remembered.

"That was different."

"I was seven. He was nine. I fell in love with him the first time I saw him. I love him still. It can happen."

She stroked her daughter's hair. "What does age

matter? Not at all. Not when something's supposed to be.''

Anna raised her head. "Supposed to be? Kent's not a cowboy, Mama. I'm not a countess."

Her mother's bright green eyes met her own. "That's not what he says."

Anna clicked her tongue against her teeth. "You sound as foolish as he does."

The sea-green irises twinkled. "'Children and fools cannot lie.'"

"Another Old Irish proverb?" Anna asked.

"English, I believe."

Anna looked away. "He's crazy." She could still feel her mother's eyes on her.

"I don't know why I didn't see it sooner. All those years..." Her mother's voice dropped. "Sure, I had my own sorrowful heart, but I thought your sadness was from the poverty, the shame...."

Anna looked at her mother. "I had no reason to be ashamed, Mama. Neither of us did."

She stroked Anna's cheek. "No, you were only brokenhearted. You belonged somewhere else, with someone else. You dated others, even almost married, but you couldn't, could you? You've always known it. Now I know it. And so does he. You belong to K.C."

Anna turned away from her mother's touch. She knew her mother thought of her own husband killed twenty-seven years ago. "There is no K.C."

"Yes, there is. He's standing in the other room, waiting for his countess."

She met her mother's gaze. "There's no countess."

"She's right before me."

Anna stared into those luxuriant green eyes and saw the fertile dreams beyond. A practical woman in most aspects, her mother had not escaped her ancestors' love of romantic lore and legend. She also had her own romance to remember. So fortified, she brooked no argument.

Her mother was smiling now. Tales were spinning. "You've known it, haven't you, darling…since you were a child. I understand. Now, so does he. And he's come to be with you."

"Mama, you're crazier than he is. Didn't you hear him? He thinks he's K. C. Cowboy again?"

Her mother laughed softly, her breasts, large enough to comfort the whole world, gently rising and falling. "Lord, he was such a fierce tyke. The bruises he used to get from those silver six-shooters banging his bony hips. And the time he tried to lasso his mother's prize Persian?"

Anna had to smile. "Would've hog-tied her, too, if the cook hadn't seen him out the kitchen window."

"And you, missy, wrapped in a stained linen tablecloth, a foil tiara on your head and your hair halfway down your back, red and blond as the day's beginning. No wonder he fell in love with you."

Anna stopped smiling. "Mama, I'm not a countess. He's not a cowboy."

Her mother tilted her head, regarded her daughter. "Close your eyes, Anna. See with your heart."

She stared at her mother. "Close my eyes? In a world gone crazy?"

Her mother smiled. "Love is crazy, angel." She lowered her voice to a conspirator's hush. "It's a big part of its appeal."

"Great. I've got one nut out there with a former roller derby diva. I've got another nut in here with me."

Her mother smiled serenely.

"You're actually enjoying this. Crazy isn't funny, Ma. Crazy can be dangerous."

Her mother was still smiling. "Go see him."

Beyond the door came Ronnie's voice. "Steer wrestling? That's a day in the park compared to stepping in the rink with Attila the Honey of the Trenton Turbos."

Anna stood up.

"Are you going to him now, child?"

"I'm going out there before Ronnie gets her skates and shows him her patented 'Jackhammer' jump."

"What are you going to say to him?"

She set her hands on her hips. "Hello. Long time no see. You may think you're a cowboy named K.C. and I'm a countess, but you've obviously suffered some kind of temporary break with objective reality. You're Kent Landover, head of one of the fastest-rising computer companies in the country, a self-proclaimed workaholic and a man who was quoted as saying his planned marriage to a member of the company's board, Hilary Fairchild, will be 'a consensual merger that will benefit both their professional and personal lives.'"

Her mother rested her chin on her fist. "You've been keeping a scrap book."

Anna ignored the remark. "Then I'm going to ask Mr. Landover to give me his psychiatrist's beeper number and, depending on freeway traffic, we'll have this all resolved in less than thirty minutes."

Her mother looked up at her. "This man couldn't have come a moment too soon."

Anna rolled her eyes. "I give up." She started toward the door.

Her mother called her name. She looked back.

"You've read the articles, seen the news reports about Kent?"

"How can you miss them?" she defended.

"He looks like he's a man who has everything, doesn't he?"

She shrugged. "Certainly more than most. He always had."

"Then why do you suppose a man who has it all wants only to be a cowboy in love with you?"

"I told you. He's crazy."

"Is he?"

"Yes." She reached for the doorknob, but didn't turn it.

"It's okay to be afraid, darling." Anna heard the gentle smile in her mother's voice.

She sighed. "I'm not afraid. I'm trying to determine the best way to handle this situation. How's he look?"

"Like a man besotted."

"You're not making this any easier."

"Nothing worthwhile ever is, child—especially love."

Anna leveled a stern look at her mother. "How's he look?"

Her mother chuckled. "A whole heck of a lot better than you, Countess."

Anna looked down at her clothes still covered with spots of something dark that smelled like anchovies. She picked at a suspicious yellowish-brown dried smear.

She looked back over her shoulder at her mother. "Some countess, huh?"

Her mother was still smiling that infuriating smile. "Wait until you see the cowboy."

Anna reclaimed her hold on the door handle. "For the final time, Ma. There's no countess. There's no cowboy."

She said it so convincingly, she almost believed it herself. She twisted the doorknob and opened the door as if ready for what lay on the other side.

She saw him. At the same time he saw her. He stood, but didn't step farther. She, too, stopped. She'd seen the pictures throughout the years—the publicity that came with being the son of a wealthy, well-connected family, then an entity in his own right. The photos showcased a serious child, a serious youth, and finally, a serious man. He kept his curly blond hair cropped short, his clothes conservative and tailored. She hadn't seen one picture of him smiling.

He came toward her now, his smile so broad and full of life, she had to smile back.

He took her hands in both of his. Not until his fingers found hers did she realize she was trembling.

"Anna" was all he said. Then again, "Anna." Impossible as it seemed, his smile widened even farther. Suddenly her whole world was in that smile...and went no further.

She looked up into his eyes. Those she remembered most of all. She saw again the ever-present intelligence, the piercing blue, the sky, the sea and all dreams in between.

For a moment, one mad moment, she believed he could be K.C.

She disentangled their hands, stepped back. She saw the dark green hospital scrubs he wore.

"Kent," she said.

He raised a finger to her lips. "No. K.C. Surely you remember?"

Yes, she remembered. She'd never forgotten. His finger touched her cheek now. She raised her hand and captured his touch in her own. He held to her fast.

"K.C.," she allowed. "What are you doing here?"

His gaze remained on her. "I've come for you, Anna. Marry me. Be my bride."

She heard the words as she'd heard them so many times in her imaginings. She looked into his eyes, crescent shaped, cobalt ringed. She'd say yes. She'd promise him anything. Just let him look at her like that for the rest of her life.

"Marry me, Anna."

How, with one look, one touch and a few words, had he wrapped her within his illusion? How could she see K.C. before her when he'd barely existed before, had never been more than the play of childhood, the brief, bold vision of youth?

She was shocked back to simple reality. Kent Landover was before her now. K.C. was gone, might never have been. And she was left as crazy as her mother, as crazy as this man.

She stepped back once more, putting distance between them. His hand tightened on her fingers. She saw his oversize scrubs. What she'd thought were beige loafers she now saw were foam rubber slip-ons. The uniform of the institutionalized. How had this happened? Why? When?

She looked back up into his eyes. He'd come to her. She'd help him. That she could do.

She took a step toward him. Again she wondered what had happened to him to cause such a complete break with reality.

"Kent?"

"K.C.," he softly insisted.

"K.C." She obliged. "Those are rather unusual clothes for a cowboy."

He looked down at his outfit. "Please pardon my attire, Anna," he said with such sincere formality, a bit of her heart chipped away. "I was in the hospital…"

Her heart broke.

"They wanted to keep me there. They didn't believe me when I said I felt fine, actually never better. They said my head was hurt. I've a bump, a few bruises from the blackout, but nothing to keep a man locked up.''

Now there was no doubt. He had been institutionalized. The reality of it was worse than she'd imagined.

''Then I saw you on the TV…'' he was saying.

Those commercials she'd done for the cleaning business.

''I couldn't find my clothes anywhere, so I borrowed these from the hospital. I'm going to return them as soon as I find mine.''

''Of course.'' She nodded.

''I couldn't wait another minute. I've been looking for you for a long time, Anna. Ever since you left.''

She tried to smile. ''Now you've found me.''

''We'll never be apart again, Anna. Never.''

She felt the constriction building through her body. Soon it would require release in tears or screams or a blank, unseeing stare out a window for a long, still moment.

HE LOOKED INTO HER FACE, wishing her thoughts were his. He'd been too abrupt, he thought. He'd been clumsy, raw, spitting proposals at her like a sailor newly dry-docked. She was scared. He could see it in the white circles of her eyes.

He looked away from the crown the color of pale amber and the eyes he'd made large by his rush of words. He looked down, seeing his ill-fitting pajamas worn from too many washings, and felt the fool. He'd seen her, and from that moment on, there'd been nothing else. He'd come like a man possessed, single-minded in pursuit. She, so nobly bred, had been too gracious to show her real response. God, he was as simple as the land and the life he loved. She must think him crazy.

He looked back up into those white-ringed eyes that reflected his own fearful heart. "I'm not crazy."

There was no more than a blink, delicate as a fairy wing. Her mouth opened. He waited for her words bringing either condemnation or resurrection, but she said nothing. He watched the lips curve like a new bud unfurling. He didn't have to touch his own lips to know a smile had found its way there, too.

He wasn't quite sure if he'd been accepted or absolved. He wasn't certain about a lot of things. He didn't know why others kept confusing him with another man, a strange man who shared his name but nothing else. He didn't know why he thought he, no more than a cowboy, could win the affections of a countess. There were a lot of things he was uncertain about. Some moments were even downright shaky. Things he had an idea he'd once believed and understood now made no sense. He didn't understand his ease traveling through the streets of this strange city. Nor did he understand the sudden flash of images in his mind, so different from the life that he knew was his. Then, at times, there was nothing—a complete blank...save for Anna. Anna was the one constant.

"K.C." The sweet voice of his salvation pulled

him from his whirl of thoughts. He looked and found the cool, green rest of her eyes. Everything that had seemed senseless made sense once more.

She gave his hand a squeeze. "Let's go have tea and Mama's scones."

She led him, and he had a sense of being very young and very happy for no reason other than being near her. A sense that those same words, these same steps in perfect rhythm, her hand held tight in his, had all happened before. Once upon a time.

"Anna?"

She stopped and turned toward him, smiling that smile he'd also seen before, would remember forever.

"I may be a little crazy."

Those eyes welled into wide rings again, the colors brightening as if wet. Her hand dropped his. As her fingers pulled away, his own still reached out. She stepped toward him, laid her cheek against his in the briefest of moments and whispered, "Me, too."

She stepped back and took the fingers that had never stopped reaching for her. She smiled. "Come on, cowboy."

HER MOTHER FED HIM SCONES and tea, and Anna excused herself to take a shower. But first she slipped back down the stairs to the reception area. Ronnie glanced up from the morning paper as Anna came into the room.

"How's our cowboy?"

"'Our' cowboy? Weren't you the one a few

minutes ago sizing him up for a Square Rock Stomp?''

Ronnie smiled. ''Any guy who can look at you like that when you smell of herring can't be all bad.''

Anna shook her head. ''Kent Landover.''

She was about to flop down into a chair when Ronnie cautioned, ''Not the crushed velour.''

She straightened and, folding her arms, leaned against the wall, staring forward, not seeming to see.

''I didn't know your mother and you had such impressive connections.'' Ronnie laid thick her accent.

''Mom worked for the Landover family for four years.''

''No kidding?''

''It was years ago. I was a baby. Mama wasn't much more than a child herself, nineteen. She'd met my father in her first foster home. He'd shown her the ropes, protected her. They were separated, but as soon as he could, he came for her. They married and came to California to start a new life together. He was killed in a car accident not long after I was born.'' Anna's voice dropped. ''Mama never loved another.''

She gathered memories. ''After my father's death, Mama got a job on the Landovers' household staff. She was lucky. The position didn't pay much, but it included room and board. We lived on the estate, in the back, in a cottage with gingerbread trim.''

Her thoughts drifted further. ''Kent was about two years older than me. An only child, he'd been left to the care of nannies and nurses since he was born. His parents were busy people. His father had his business, his mother her charities and social intrigues. I was Kent's first real friend, and he, mine. His parents didn't approve of the friendship. I was a servant's child. They spoke to my mother, but when Kent came to our cottage, a lonely child wanting to play, Mama didn't have the heart to send him away. Sometimes, when Mama was working and Kent's parents weren't home, we'd even play at the big house. Games children play—hide-and-seek, 'Mother, May I...?'''

"Dress-up?" Ronnie asked.

Anna nodded. "It was our favorite. He was always K. C. Cowboy; I was always—"

"The Countess." Ronnie understood.

Anna had to smile, remembering. "We were happy. Mom was happy, too. She sewed curtains for the cottage, embroidered pillowcases for our beds. She'd never had a real home, but this came close. She had a small salary and a roof over our heads, and, as time went on, I didn't hear her crying so much in the night. Everything was pretty perfect. I thought it would stay that way forever. I was young."

"What happened?"

"We would play dress-up and pretend for hours. Sometimes Kent would bring things from the big house for the dress-up box—a scarf, a hat, a necklace, a bracelet. We only saw pretty colors, sparkling stones, tinted lights. I didn't know until later the jewelry was real. I didn't know its value. I kept them, thousands of dollars of precious gems, in a box in the back of my closet with a tinfoil tiara and a toy six-shooter set. When they were found, my mother was as shocked as the Landovers. I told them I didn't know the jewelry was worth so much money. I told them I'd only borrowed it for dress-up. The Landovers didn't press charges, but we had to leave immediately.''

"But when Kent explained how—?"

"I never told anyone Kent had brought the jewelry. I didn't want to get him into trouble. I was afraid they wouldn't let him have any more friends, and he'd be all alone again, like he was before I came. I was five. He was seven.

"We had each other. The rest of the world was ruled by adults who decided what had happened and what would be done. We were only children.''

Her throat tightened. "I never got a chance to say goodbye.''

Ronnie's eyes widened. "Hold on. The last time you saw this guy, you were five?"

Anna nodded.

"And he walks in here this morning and proposes marriage?" Ronnie shook her head. "He's cute, but he's got to be crazy.''

"He said he'd come from the hospital. The back of his shirt says Property of UCLA Medical Center. I came down to check if there was something about an accident or a missing person in the paper this morning. You didn't see anything, did you?"

"Yeah, right here, on the first page of the business section—Kent Landover Goes Loony Tunes.''

"I'm only trying to figure this out.''

"Honey, if something did happen, they're not going to issue a press release and start a panicked sell-off of Landover Tech stock. I'd say start with UCLA."

"I suppose they might be able to explain everything." Anna sighed. "I'm not sure I want to know. Kent Landover...crazy?"

"I've seen crazier on Hollywood Boulevard in broad daylight," Ronnie said as she went back to scanning the paper. "Maybe he didn't escape from the loony bin. Maybe he got a batch of mad cow beef. Wait—" Ronnie's finger stopped halfway down the newspaper page. "There's something here about Landover Technology."

"What?" Anna rounded the desk and looked over Ronnie's shoulder.

"Never mind. Nothing helpful. Speculation about a possible partnership with some Asian company," Ronnie said, reading. She glanced up at Anna. "You think our cowboy upstairs is interested?"

She shook her head. "Not at the moment."

They heard the sound of footsteps coming down the stairs. As the back door to the reception area opened, Maureen was saying, "Are you sure you don't want to lie down a spell, K.C.? Your body is still recovering from your accident yesterday."

"He only lost it yesterday?" Ronnie whispered to Anna. "And the first thing he does is come looking for you? Can you say 'stalker'?"

"S-s-s-h-h!" Anna hushed her.

Kent was holding the door open for Anna's mother.

"Ma'am," he said to her, "I don't believe I've ever felt better in my entire life." He turned and smiled at Anna.

"Tea and scones." He looked toward the window. "Sunshine." His gaze went back to Anna. "And finding the sweetest little gal ever to set foot down on God's good earth. That's all an ailing man needs."

Anna mustered a wan smile.

"Whoa, cowboy." Ronnie laughed. "You sure do know how to shoot the—"

"Ronnie." Maureen cut her off. She looked at the two women. "Anna, you haven't even taken a shower yet? The new girls will be here for orientation in thirty minutes. I would prefer my head trainer doesn't smell like fish."

"I was on my way…but then…" She paused, saw Kent eyeing the monitor on the desk. "Ronnie needed help…rebooting the computer."

"Rebooting?" Kent walked over to the desk. "I've heard of reshoeing, but never rebooting." He stood next to her, stared down at the computer screen.

"Come on," Ronnie protested. "You practically invented—"

"You don't know much about computers, K.C.?" Anna interrupted.

He was still studying the screen. "Tell you the truth, darn fangled things scare me to death."

Anna looked at Ronnie.

Ronnie pantomimed picking up a phone and dialing. "Call the hospital pronto," she mouthed.

Chapter Three

Anna pulled the quilt up closer to Kent's throat. Despite his protests, fatigue had overcome him by mid-afternoon, and he'd relented to Maureen's urgings to "get a little rest." Anna came upstairs to check on him ten minutes later, and he was already asleep, his lips curved, smiling at his dreams.

Free from watching eyes, she stared at his face, resisting the urge to touch the cheek dark with a day's beard. Her heart rose and fell with the movement of his chest. How long had she dreamed one day he'd walk through her door, throw his arms around her and carry her off to a world of their own? How many hours had she imagined watching him as she watched him now, seeing him sleep and knowing his dreams would be of her? How long had the thought of him formed the foundation of her everyday existence?

Forever, her heart whispered.

Her hand rose, her fingertips hovering where his brow met blond curls beginning. The brow was almost smooth now, padded by a slight swell. The long-formed furrows were no more than thin lines. She saw a bruise blending beneath the day's beard.

Whether he was crazy or not, she'd like to think she'd brought him happiness for brief moments. For he hadn't been happy. She knew. She'd seen him happy once. She hadn't seen the same light in his eyes for a long time. At first she'd thought it was the grainy newsprint or the artificial pose of a publicity shot. But gradually she'd realized it wasn't the picture. It was the man. There was no joy in his features.

Until today.

So she sat inches from the only man she'd ever loved and hoped these short hours together were hours of happiness. She couldn't, didn't dare to hope for more. For those eyes, closed now, would one day open and no longer see K. C. Cowboy, no longer see Countess Anna. They'd see Kent Coleman Landover, CEO, board chairman. They'd see Anna Delaney, clean queen. One day the man would wake.

Their worlds had met, aligned once, a long time ago, when they were both unaware of bloodlines or bank accounts. It had ended swiftly. It would end again. The first time, she hadn't known, and so could be forgiven.

The second time would be pure foolishness.

She rose wearily, suddenly tired herself. She'd postponed calling the hospital, using the excuse of the morning orientation session, then the welcome flurry of phone inquiries. She'd been stalling for time. She left Kent still sleeping, still smiling.

She went into the downstairs conference room, shut

the door and dialed. As an electronic voice listed her choice of options, she realized she was uncertain whom she should talk to. Given the public and professional interest surrounding Kent, one word to the wrong person and she risked damaging his reputation and the credibility of his company.

She disconnected and stared down at the receiver. Should she call his office? The company's powers-that-be must be aware of Kent's current condition, and, for the good of the company if nothing else, could be counted on for discretion. The receiver's dial tone began to beep. She punched in Directory Assistance and got the number for Landover Technology.

She asked to be connected to Kent Landover's office, hoping to speak to whoever was steering the ship while the captain played cowboy. When a woman answered, "Mr. Landover's office," Anna gave her name and asked to speak to him. The woman hesitated, then asked what the call was in reference to.

Anna simply said, "K.C."

A man's voice came on the line immediately. "What'd you say your first name was?"

"Anna."

The man moaned. "The countess?"

She was uncertain how to reply.

"This just keeps getting better and better."

"Who am I speaking to?" Anna asked.

"No. Who am I speaking to?" the man countered.

"I told you my name is Anna Delaney—"

"The countess?"

"No, well, not exactly."

"This is wonderful. This is rich. Miriam?" the man yelled. Anna pulled the phone away from her ear. "Where's my Tagamet?"

Without taking a breath, the man demanded, "What exactly is the nature of your current relationship with Kent Landover?"

"I don't have a current relationship with Kent Landover—"

"But you did?"

"Yes...once...but it was a very long time ago."

"What was it? A back-seat session in the limo after your coming-out ball? A fling in between semesters at Stanford? That weekend conference in Tahoe? Miriam, the Tagamet!"

Anna struggled to keep her tone controlled. "I'd like to speak to someone else, please."

"No, sister. I'm your best bet. First of all, only a handful of others know about this situation, but they all have valid incentives to want to keep it that way. However, I doubt the motives of a one-night stand called The Countess. Unless you can fax me the family tree, I say you're not even royalty."

"I'm not." Anna could almost hear the man's blood pressure rising. "I'm also not a one-night stand."

"Ha! Listen, lady, I don't care what kind of relationship you had with Kent. In fact, I don't even want to know, but if it could threaten the reputation of Kent Landover and this company, I'll make it my business to know. I'll dig up every time you so much as crossed against the light if I have to. Then try to go public with the story of your meaningless little affair with Kent. Just try. Do you really think they'll listen to someone who goes by the name The Countess?''

''Probably not.''

''Probably...not.'' She'd stopped the man cold. ''Still, you're still planning to go to the papers with your story?''

''Of course not.''

''Of course...not,'' he parroted again, puzzled. ''What do you want, then?''

''I called to tell you that Mr. Landover is here with me.''

''Good God!'' His voice burst through the speaker. ''You've kidnapped him.''

Anna waited a second, then put the phone back to her ear.

The man was still talking, threatening. ''...and I'll hunt you down and personally throttle you with—''

''I did not kidnap Mr. Landover.'' Anna made each word distinct. Her initial indignation, however, was tempered by the concern she heard in the man's voice.

''No, he just signed himself out of the hospital and walked in your door this morning?''

''Is that what the hospital told you? When did they start letting patients sign themselves out of the psychiatric ward?''

''Psychiatric ward?'' The phone in Anna's hand vibrated. ''He wasn't in the psychiatric ward. He's not crazy.''

''I see.'' The more enraged the man's voice became, the calmer Anna kept her responses. "Then the cowboy thing is a midlife career change?"

There was a pause, then the man said, "Kent Landover had an accident yesterday. He swerved to avoid hitting a bus and lost control of his vehicle. Fortunately, he only suffered a concussion. Unfortunately, as a result of the head injury, he has amnesia."

"Amnesia." She said it once, then twice more as if the word had magical powers. "That's wonderful."

"I wouldn't go that far."

"He's not crazy?"

"Believe me, Kent Landover is the sanest, most sensible man I know, and I can assure you, and the doctors can assure you, he'll return to that sane, sensible man any minute now. But until then, he believes he's a cowboy named K.C. in love with a countess named Anna."

"I know." She spoke quietly.

"Ms...?"

"Delaney," she again filled in.

"Ms. Delaney, my name is Leon Skow. I'm executive vice president and one of the original investors in Landover Technology. I'm also Kent's friend. I'm beginning to think you are, too. Am I right?"

"Yes."

"Good. Then maybe you'd like to tell me how you fit into all this?"

Leon listened in rare silence as she explained everything. He didn't speak again until she was at the part when she'd decided to call Landover Tech instead of the UCLA Medical Center.

"How'd you know he'd come from the medical center?"

"Their name was stamped on his scrubs."

"He's wearing scrubs?"

"And foam rubber slippers."

"He walked through the streets of L.A. like that?"

"I'm sure no one even noticed. After all, this is L.A."

"Do you know if he's talked to anyone else besides you?"

"My mother and Ronnie were here when he came in this morning."

Leon moaned.

"Don't worry," she assured him. "My mother doesn't think he's crazy. She thinks he's finally come to his senses. After some initial resistance, I think he's charmed Ronnie, also."

"Who's Ronnie? Your boyfriend?"

"No, Ronnie's our receptionist. Her real name is Veronica, but 'Ronnie, the Bam Bam Bomber' played better in the roller derby circuit."

"Exactly what kind of a business do you run, Ms. Delaney?"

"Call me Anna. My mother just opened a cleaning service. The Clean Queens. Perhaps you've heard of us?"

There was silence, then Leon was chuckling. "I think I've heard of you."

"Really? We wanted a name that'd attract attention."

"I think you accomplished that."

"We've been advertising, of course. Newspapers, a billboard, couple of late-night TV spots—"

"Buses?" Leon asked.

"You've seen the ads?"

"Not me. Someone else."

"We're trying to hit the ground running, if you know what I mean."

"These ads?" Leon asked. "They show a woman with a crown?"

"I've got a feather-duster scepter, too."

"You're the woman in the ads?"

"As a former roller derby champion, Ronnie thought it was beneath her dignity."

"Now I understand." Leon relayed to Anna everything Kent had remembered right before the accident.

"Seeing you on the back of the bus must've triggered some long-buried memory in his mind," he concluded. "I wouldn't even be surprised if now that he's seen you, his memory comes back. What's he doing now?"

"Sleeping."

"Sleeping? Good. Sleep is good. Why, he could wake up right this very second and be back to his old self. And all this nonsense will be over."

Anna heard the hope in Leon's voice.

"Any minute now, everything could be back to normal. Give me your address, and I'll be right over to get him."

She recited her address.

"And Anna," Leon cautioned before hanging up, "keep an eye on him. The CEO of Landover Technology wandering about L.A. in pajamas and slippers isn't exactly the image the company wants to project.''

She promised, hung up the phone and went out to the reception area. Ronnie was taking a call. Anna's mother was on-site with a new group of girls. Anna started toward the stairs.

At the doorway, she heard Ronnie say, ''How's our cowboy?''

Anna turned around. ''I spoke with a vice president at Landover Technology. Kent had a car accident yesterday. He has amnesia.''

''Amnesia?''

Anna nodded. ''Right before the accident he saw me in a Clean Queens ad. Seeing the ad, then taking the blow to his head somehow altered his memory. When he woke up, he believed K. C. Cowboy and the Countess were real. It makes perfect sense.''

''I suppose—''

''Of course it does.'' She wasn't going to allow any alternative speculations. She'd already heard enough nonsense about destiny and fate and the power of true love.

''The man has a big bump on his head. It's as simple as that.'' She started again toward the stairs, ending the discussion. She made her steps on the stairs quick and light.

He was still sleeping, smiling. Again she pulled the quilt up to his neck, even though she knew the gesture was done more for her than him. The comfortably warm temperature in the room made any covers unnecessary. She would go now. Soon, so would he.

She had even taken a step when his hand closed around her wrist and pulled her back, landing her in the curve of his resting body, his mouth meeting hers in a movement fluid, fine, like the first taste of wind.

Another's breath, another's being, one she had longed for her whole life, found her and filled her. She felt her lips widen, her need expanding, grasping. He touched his tongue to her, and her need breathed, ballooned, banishing all else. Reason, protest, rationale, all to blackness.

She went to him, pressing close to the reclining angle of his body, feeling the warmth of his body through the thin shirt. She lay full on the hard relief of his chest, feeling the sheer solidity of him, reveling in the cocoon of his arms. *Hold me,* she prayed, even then, in the delirium of her desire, hearing the folly of her thoughts. Still, her incantation played: *Don't let me go. Don't let me go.*

She bid his tongue into her mouth, the press of her body matching the press of her desire. Her hands found his face. As she touched the day-old beard shadowing his cheeks, she smiled beneath the circle of his lips. Her fingertips feathered across his forehead, arced across his eyes closed to the world. There was only her; there was only him. She drew her fingertip across one blond brow, then the other, needing to touch, to feel, to remember.

Her hands moved on, touching each temple, the beginning border of thick curls. One hand threaded through the wave to curve about that magnificent blond crown. The other passed again across his forehead, feeling the slight swell of skin there, remembering, remembering too much.

She sat up. Her hands touched him a second longer as if her responses had slowed, and her very body was denying her demands. She stood up, angry only with herself. She turned her back to him. Her eyes closed, seeking once more the blackness, but this time, the blackness of complete control.

It came, so that when he stood and touched her back, she was able to silently step away.

"Anna?"

Such a sweet voice, she thought. She alone could hear the child in it. The child she had known. Sometimes before, when there had been only pictures to indulge her foolish fantasies, she had looked hard, seeking the child. Beneath the sharp lines of tailored suits, the determined angles of his profile, the slashes drawn across his brow, slanting down his cheeks, she looked and there was the child. She would peer closely, remembering the boy, the smile willing, the body knobby and awkward before the hardness and denial had drawn it up stiff. She remembered herself and him and the happiness they alone believed possible.

And now, finally, although it made no sense and would be short-lived, so had he. It was enough to allow her to smile and, smiling still, turn and face him.

She hadn't been prepared for the confusion, the despair she saw on his face. His hands were lifted to her, offering, entreating.

"Anna, I love you. Is it wrong?"

She took those hands in hers, but when he began to step toward her, she tightened her hold, halting him.

"Let's sit down," she said, leading him back to the couch still warm from their presence.

"Kent—" she began.

"K.C." he insisted.

"K.C." she started again, concentrating on his face, keeping her voice kind, "I spoke with the vice president of Landover Technology a little while ago."

He looked at her, puzzled.

"Leon," she said. "Leon Skow."

His brow wrinkled. "Leon," he murmured. "Short guy? Talks fast?"

She laughed. "I've never seen him in person, but he does talk fast."

He smiled. "Bit abrupt but a nice enough fella. I met him yesterday at the hospital."

"You remember?"

"Sure, he was there with some dark-haired woman." He smiled again as he remembered. "They were so confused."

"They were confused?"

He nodded. "They thought I was some other guy named Kent Landover. Some big shot here in L.A. who owns that company you mentioned."

"Landover Technology."

"That's it. He must be pretty rich."

"He is," she confirmed.

"You know him?"

She looked into the blue wash of his eyes, so clear and light, they seemed to spill silver.

"Kent…"

His eyes clouded to the color of shadows on snow.

"Anna, we need to talk about us," he said. "Not these strangers."

"They aren't strangers, Kent."

Despite the tight hold she had on his hands, he pulled free. "K.C., Anna," he pleaded. "I'm K.C."

"Leon told me you had an accident yesterday."

"I told you that, too." He stood and went to the window as she'd done only moments ago. It was his time to turn his back.

"That's right, you did. You said you hurt your head but you're fine now."

"I wasn't lying to you." Small clouds formed as his breath touched the glass. "I am fine."

She stood up, took a step toward him. "Do you remember the doctors saying you had amnesia?"

He turned. "I know you're worried, but there's nothing wrong with me, Anna. I love you. I can take care of you and make you happy."

He came to her, placing his hands on her shoulders. She looked into the silver sheen of his eyes. "Believe in me, Anna. Believe in us."

She did believe, she thought. She always had.

They stood together, the belief in themselves and what could be full in their hearts. In that moment, it was possible. Everything was possible. A computer wizard could be a wrangler. A cleaning girl could be a countess. If they believed...

"A-n-n-n-a!" Ronnie called from below. "Some people are here to see you."

She received the summons with a smile, knowing she'd been saved. She and Kent walked downstairs, still hand in hand, their descent unhurried. The ground level beckoned, but Anna's steps remained slow and measured. She would reach the flat surface soon enough.

She heard Leon even before they reached the reception room.

"Within a year, you're going to want triple the megabytes on this baby," he was telling Ronnie as he examined the back of her computer's central unit. "What speed modem do you have?"

A beautiful brunette, perched on the edge of one of the red velour chairs, jumped up.

"Kent!"

Anna recognized the woman coming toward them as Kent's fiancé. The woman scanned Kent's outfit. She hesitated. Her smile dissolved.

Leon looked up. "Buddy!" He came toward Kent, arms outstretched. "Out stalking the streets, huh? I don't blame you...not after I heard it was chipped beef on toast day at the hospital."

Leon embraced him in a back-patting hug. Kent stood, body stiff. He looked from Leon to Hilary.

"What're you doing here?" he asked. "I explained everything to you yesterday. I'm not the man you think I am."

Leon glanced at Anna.

"I called them," she said.

Kent looked at her. "Why?"

"They're very worried about you."

He glanced at Leon and Hilary again, then back at Anna.

"They're your friends. You just don't remember them."

Kent shook his head. "No, these people don't know me. Not like you do, Anna."

"You remember them with you yesterday in the hospital, don't you?"

Kent looked for a long moment at Leon and Hilary. He nodded.

"Do you remember the doctor talking about amnesia?" Leon asked.

Kent nodded, still looking at Leon and Hilary.

"Do you remember him saying the blow to your head caused a temporary memory loss?" Hilary asked.

Again he nodded.

"But there's no reason you won't fully recover in a few weeks," Anna said too brightly. "You'll be your ol' self again in no time...and everything won't seem so confusing."

Kent shifted his gaze to her. "I'm not confused, Anna."

"You left the hospital before the doctors could perform necessary tests," Leon pointed out. "They need to take X rays to determine your condition."

"My condition?"

"But all those tests can be done on an outpatient basis, darling," Hilary added. "However, you do need rest to recover fully. That the doctor was very adamant about. So we've come to take you home." She took a tentative step toward him.

"There's nothing wrong with me."

"Probably not," Anna said. The cheerleader smile had become frozen on her face. "But this way, you'll be sure."

He looked down at her. "You're worried, too?"

She nodded. Her throat had grown too tight to speak.

"You think I should go with these people?"

She swallowed hard. "You don't remember them now, but you will. They're your friends."

Kent looked about the room. "I'll go," he said. "Only because this seems a way to resolve this mix-up once and for all."

"Good choice," Leon said.

But Kent was looking at Anna. "I'll be back for you." He bent down swiftly and kissed her hard on the lips. His mouth slid to her cheek. "I'll be back," he whispered against the yield of flesh, the opening of pores.

He pulled away, turned to the two others. "Let's go."

They walked to the door. He turned only once. He looked at her.

Sound welled within her, climbed up her throat. Her mouth opened, her lips drew back. The tendons in her throat contracted. Yet no sound came.

Then he was gone.

Her mouth closed. Her lips met, their tight line echoed in her flat stare, the erect, still way she stood.

The first time, she hadn't been given the chance to say goodbye. The second time, she'd been too much the coward.

Chapter Four

The Lexus came to another upward concrete curve. Centrifugal force pulled K.C. toward the latched door. The seat belt pushed against his chest. Hilary sat strapped beside him. She gave him a wide smile, her teeth white pearls echoed in the beads wrapped around her throat.

K.C. turned his head and saw the shiny skeleton of L.A. below. Soaring bends of concrete arched over one another, while others seeped ground-level—supine planes of highway meeting, then moving on, smooth, glossy with traffic.

The car crested the incline. Leon braked hard, throwing K.C. forward. Before them was a white, sterile structure, frozen even in the strong L.A. shimmer.

K.C. studied the building. The words *cold, clinical* came to his mind. Where had they brought him? Why? He had agreed to undergo the recommended tests, but it was his understanding they were to be done at the UCLA Medical Center. The fortress before him, with its blank walls and flat top, had more the look of a prison.

He glanced at Hilary, seeing her white smile. He looked front, seeing the flushed ripple of skin rimming the back of Leon's collar.

As if feeling eyes upon him, Leon twisted around and grinned at K.C. from over the seat's leather curve. "Here we are."

K.C. looked to the low, white rise before them, then back at his escorts. Nothing looked familiar.

Hilary laid a cool palm on his forearm. "Shall we go inside, darling?"

He stepped out of the car into the thinned air and walked with Hilary and Leon to the white box of a building, its corners sharpened by the sun's albino sheen.

Inside was as unrelieved as the outside. Great walls of unbroken white, cool, uncovered floors of pale maple, broad, boxy furniture. No baseboards, no moldings, no lamps, no drapes. Everything had been stripped to its barest possibilities.

Hilary and Leon followed as he walked from room to room, touching the angular arm of a chair, a metal sculpture. There were no pictures of people, no plants, no pets. Nothing was soft beneath his fingertips.

He looked back to Leon and Hilary, and they'd dissolved, their forms blotted out beneath the fierce light coming into the room at all angles. K.C. shielded his eyes, squinting to find perimeters within the white void.

Leon stepped out of the flat brilliance and took

hazy shape. He spread his arms, embracing the vault-ceilinged room. "Home, sweet home."

K.C. felt the first push of panic. He wasn't expected to live in this white tomb?

"That's right generous of you offering to put me up. I don't want to act like an ungrateful saddle tramp, but once the docs pronounce me healthy, I'll be on my way again. Anna's waiting for me. So if we could go over to the hospital—"

"Kent, this is your house," Hilary said. She walked the length of an ivory couch, running her hand across its edge. "All of it."

Even his laugh sounded lifeless in the vast room. "My house?" Again his laugh mocked him.

"You designed it yourself," Hilary told him.

He walked to a wide, girded window opening out onto a cast-concrete deck. A low fence of white steel tubing compressed a hillside of dusty dried grass.

Who was this man they thought he was? This man who would live up here, high, alone in the flat, white light, surrounded by sharp edges and hard surfaces?

There was a touch on his shoulder. He looked at Leon. The man's ruddy complexion could have been seared by the light.

"Don't worry, buddy. Now that we've got you back in your own home, a few days rest and you'll be ready to take on the world again."

"This isn't my house."

Hilary was at his other side. "You don't remember, darling. It's the amnesia."

"No, it's not the amnesia. My home is with Anna."

A look passed between Hilary and Leon.

"Why don't we sit down?" Hilary suggested.

He let himself be led to the long, dominating sofa. He shouldn't have left Anna. Everything made sense when he was with her. Away from her, everything became confused.

Hilary sat down, patted the leather surface next to her, her eyes sharp on K.C. Leon remained standing, but his gaze stayed on K.C., too. K.C. knew they saw a man he was not. Short of that man's return, he had no idea how to convince these people he wasn't who they wanted him to be.

All he knew was he had to get back to Anna.

Perhaps, if he played along, pretended to be this odd fellow they thought he was, the quicker they would leave him alone. And the quicker he could get back to Anna.

He let his gaze sweep the room once more, then pause at a dark-framed painting. He stared for several seconds too long.

Hilary followed the direction of his study. "What is it?" Her voice lost some of its smooth varnish. "Do you recognize the Oppenheim? Lord knows you were angry enough when that South Bay swank tried to outbid you for it."

"I'm not sure," he replied. "There's something…"

Leon's hand clapped his shoulder. "A few days in your own environment, and you'll be back to your ol'

self, skipper. Take my word for it. We probably
would've been better off taking you down to the office instead of here. That's your real home. Don't
worry. Tomorrow morning, Hilary is going to take
you for your tests, and when you're finished, you can
swing by the office and see if anything rings a bell.
Maybe that redhead who started last week in market-
ing, huh?'' Leon winked.

"Redhead?'' K.C. beetled his brow and concentrated as if he was trying to remember.

Hilary slid her arm through his and pulled him to
her reedlike figure. "Don't strain yourself, darling.''
She shifted her gaze. "Leon, speaking of the office,
shouldn't you be getting back?''

"Subtle, Hilary...but true.'' Leon patted K.C.
twice on the shoulder. "You rest and get better,
buddy. We need you in tip-top form when the Sushima people come in next week. Bring him by the office
tomorrow,'' he said to Hilary. "It'll be good for
him.''

"I'll walk you out.'' Hilary rose and left the room
with Leon, their voices blended in low conversation.

K.C. smiled. He'd gotten rid of one of them already.

Hilary returned to the room, her broad smile split-
ting at the corners. She came toward the couch.
"Don't worry, darling. You may have forgotten a lot
of things, but I'll make sure you don't forget you're
a soon-to-be-married man.''

"Are you and I in love?''

She stopped midstep. Her smile stayed wide, but

he saw her swallow. Her hand rose, curved through the air. "What a question." Her laughter was the tinkling of high notes.

"You said we were to be married?"

"Yes, you asked me to marry you."

"How'd I do it?"

"How'd you do it?" She was walking now in small steps around the room, straightening some books already fanned out across a chiseled stone table.

"Did I bring you flowers and champagne, bend down on one knee?"

Her bubble of laughter rose and broke throughout the room. "Hardly."

"Tell me, then. Maybe the description of such an important moment will jar my memory."

Her laughing countenance sobered. "Your lawyers faxed the offer to my lawyers. Once a prenuptial agreement was reached by both parties, we signed on the dotted lines."

K.C. looked at her, his incredulity real. "That's it?"

"I believe the lawyers got a little weepy over the thought of their fabulous fees." Hilary pantomimed a smile.

K.C. continued to stare at her in disbelief.

"We're realists, Kent, not romantics. You'll remember soon enough. Until then, it's wise to take my word for it. I'm going to have a mineral water before dinner. Would you like something?"

He shook his head. Hilary glided through the room's emptiness and left.

Alone, K.C. shook his head once more. Marriage proposals outlined by lawyers? A house like a blank abyss? A climate-controlled office as the perfect antidote?

No wonder this Kent fellow had run away.

K.C. LEANED BACK in the black leather chair and stretched his legs across the teak wood desk. The morning had been spent at the hospital, but the preliminary results had shown no physical abnormalities. K.C. ran his hands along the underneath of the chair's padded arms, hoping for a vibrating-massage button. No luck. He wasn't surprised. From what he knew, this Kent fellow didn't seem like the vibrating-massage type.

After the hospital, Hilary had taken him to a restaurant where everyone kissed everyone else on the cheek. Then she'd brought him to this office. He was still continuing his charade of attempting to remember in an effort to appease Hilary and Leon. He must be convincing—at brief instances, certain images or ideas even struck him as familiar. The restaurant, of course, was world renowned so he could have seen it in a movie or a magazine. And aren't most maître d's named Claude? And if he was the hotshot Hilary and Leon kept insisting he was, his office couldn't be anywhere else but the top floor, and that would explain how he'd automatically pressed the right button when they'd stepped into the elevator.

He looked down the length of his outstretched legs. Those loafers with the silly tassels Hilary insisted were his favorites weren't familiar. For that much he was grateful. Being closed up in a building where the windows didn't open was equally unfamiliar and doubly irritating.

Pointing one tasseled foot, he pushed off and whirled around and around in the high-backed chair.

"Whee-e-e-e-e!"

"Mr. Landover?"

"Yes?" He grabbed hold of the desk edge. His gaze realigned until there was only one of his secretary, Mrs. Winifred Staub.

He smiled. She didn't. It didn't surprise him. He hadn't noticed many smiles since he'd come into this building. In fact, most people seemed more frightened of him than friendly.

"What a rush," he declared. "Would you like to try it?" He jumped up and stood behind the chair, swiveling it right and left. He waited for a smile.

"No, thank you, Mr. Landover."

"Are you sure?" He continued the chair's tempting dance. "I'll give you a good push-off."

She stared at him, her eyes tiny behind much too large black-framed lenses. "Quite sure."

She walked briskly into the room and set a neat pile of papers on the desk's polished surface. "These require your signature when time permits."

"Have you ever sat in this chair, Winnie? It's a miracle of modern manufacturing."

The secretary jabbed at the heavy glasses that had slipped down her nose. "Not to be impertinent, Mr. Landover—"

"Winnie, Winnie, Winnie." He shook his head. "All this formality. It's as useless as teats on a bull. Now, please, call me by my first name."

She looked at him, jabbed at her glasses out of reflex.

"You were saying…" he prodded.

"Mr. Landover—"

He held up his hand. "Teats on a bull, Winnie."

"I realize you're recovering from a recent trauma—"

"Trauma, shauma. To tell you the truth, Winnie darlin', I don't think I've ever felt better. In fact…" K.C. sat down in the chair and, arms outstretched, began to spin again. "I feel like a new m-a-a-a-an!"

By the time he spun forward again, Winnie was gone. "Good girl, Winnie," he whispered to the empty room. "Escape while you still have a chance."

He stood up, restlessness building. He walked to the window, placed his hands on the sealed glass. The smog level was low, evidenced by the rare taunting of mountain peaks in the distance. He looked down to Wilshire Boulevard. Traffic was heavy; people scurrying. He looked back to the mountains, his gaze a silent human cry like a winged creature seeking shelter. And the mountains heard his call, greeted him in his own voice. He pressed his palms against the cool window.

"Get out, K.C.," he whispered. "While you still have the chance."

ANNA LIKED PHYSICAL WORK. She liked to feel the square strength of her back and the pull of muscles along the length of her legs. She didn't mind that her fingernails never grew beyond an eighth of an inch or her hair spent more time up than down. She liked knowing her shoulders could carry heavier than usual weight.

But the self-imposed pace of the past twenty-four hours had gone past the delight of hard work and was edging into physical cruelty. Still she didn't rest. Nor had she slept, unless she counted this morning when she was at the Starbucks counter, adding sugar to a double espresso, and all the surroundings had become suddenly strange. She'd gripped the counter, and even her hands had seemed to belong to someone else.

Then, in a breath, her world had returned, and the incident was blamed on her lack of sleep. She'd downed her espresso standing up, and ordered another to go. She didn't want to rest. She didn't want to be still. As long as she moved, she didn't think. As long as she didn't think, she was safe.

Deep down, she knew it was an illusion. She'd never been safe—not since that day when she'd looked into blue eyes level with hers and knew those eyes saw what she saw; knew, at night, closed, those eyes watched the same dreams.

She'd been five; Kent seven. They were children. It should've passed. It had only become stronger, and, try as she might to ignore it, subdue it, recognize the absurdity of it, it didn't matter. It was as much a truth of her life as the sun rising in the east and setting in the west. She was in love with Kent Landover.

And so her steps continued forward, and her hands constantly moved, and her thoughts were quelled beneath a frenetic mixture of motion and purpose.

That evening, when the Clean Queens' van rounded the corner too fast, with the radio playing too loud, she should have been startled to see Kent sitting on the lone step leading to her front door. She wasn't. He stood, a phoenix rising, a silhouette of Stetson and dark-clad limbs. He wasn't quite real, no more than a woman's fleeting desire once seen on a wide screen or imagined in words on a page. She stared at the image before her and knew it wasn't a hallucination. She'd known all along. Known for twenty-three years. She'd never been safe.

He watched the van pull into the narrow drive. He smiled as he started toward her.

"Anna," he called. It could've been a benediction. She swore she could feel the breeze of his voice touch her cheek. She'd stood still for thirty seconds—it was too long. Already, in that brief span, her thoughts were moving toward mutiny.

"K.C." She hadn't meant to call him, but the name was between her lips before she'd realized she'd given it voice. As if in demonic denial, it came again, softer. "K.C."

She turned away from him, opened the side panel of the van to inventory the supplies and equipment for the night crew. "Kent." She pronounced his proper name. "Do Leon and Hilary know you're here?"

"I am not a prisoner. I am not a child."

The formality of his speech drew her attention. She saw the hard stance of his body, the sudden set of his mouth, and knew she'd hurt him. Her question wasn't the greeting he'd expected. She was sorry. Still, she leveled the line of her own shoulders.

"You have amnesia, and as a result, your behavior has caused concern." Her speech adopted the same formal tone.

"Why? Because I'll sit on a big horse but not behind a big desk? Because I'd sleep better on the hard ground with only the stars above for shelter than within the white-walled prison they tell me is my home?"

His voice gentled, as did his features. "Because I'll tell a woman what's in my heart even though I know I've got no right?"

She looked at him, into those blue eyes that twenty-three years ago saw what she saw. He believed everything he said. She knew that. He believed he was a cowboy who rode the West in a world where extraordinary feats were everyday tasks, where the values of courage, honesty, integrity and conviction ruled a man's actions. She knew he believed himself in love with her.

Still, it didn't matter if he believed. It didn't matter if she believed. It wasn't the truth. He wasn't a cowboy; she wasn't a countess. It was only a matter of time, and his memory would return. He'd go back to his corporation, his fiancé. She'd remain here.

The end was as inevitable as it had been all those

years ago. Then they'd been too young to know any different. Now they were too old not to know.

She looked away from him. It was still light out, but a faint three-quarter moon had already come into the sky, promising night.

She heard his plea. "Come with me, Anna."

Oh, that moon, that shadow of light that would only grow stronger when the darkness came full. "Where would we go?"

Didn't she deserve to hear the words so that when the night grew long and black, she could look up into the moonlight and see the scene he'd paint for her now?

"We'll go up north, to the mountains where the air is cooler and the world turns silver with frost in the early morning. There'll be a creek or two, one branching off the other. Their murmur will run through our day like the blood through our body. The ridge will rise high, the valley beneath it. At night we'll lie wrapped in each other's arms, beneath the mountain's sloping shoulders."

She didn't speak, not wanting to pronounce the necessary denial. She stared into those eyes of quixotic visions, willing to believe for a minute longer. She didn't realize she was smiling until his finger touched her lips.

"I know it doesn't matter to you, but I have money."

"It doesn't matter."

"I know, but they tell me it's mine. I went to the bank, insisted they double-check that there'd been no mistake. There wasn't. I must have worked very hard or been very lucky. Perhaps both.'' He smiled.

''You don't remember at all?'' She felt her body strain toward him.

Now his hands cradled her face, and his head dipped, bringing them both into the shadow of his Stetson. The play of light and dark angled his face as if a hand run along those features would feel hills and knolls climbed and descended. She wasn't certain which drew her more—his voice, sure and unhurried; his body, strong and solid as the mountains he spoke of. Maybe it was the eyes, like a blind man just blessed with sight. She didn't know. All she knew was that she wanted to go to this man. Go to him like a child come home.

''Come with me, Anna.'' He beckoned.

There, beneath the false moon, she went. He put his mouth to hers, and her lips, already open, sought the taste of his salvation. It was wonderful and wet and she fed on those dreams, felt their heat within her, within him. She opened her mouth wider, hungry, and wrapped her arms around him, holding him to her. Still her hunger rose, needing him, needing his dreams. Gone was the world as she knew it. In its place were only two people who believed in a world of their own making, created many years ago before someone told them it couldn't be so.

The touch of skin, the taste of another was all she knew now. Her hands found his cheeks, drew him to her deeper. Her eyes were closed, and she could've been dreaming, so unreal was everything. She felt the metal of the van touch her back, the blood coming too fast within her body, the need too strong. She pressed herself to him, letting him touch her, wondering if she willed it. *Let go, let go,* she heard a voice inside, as urgent as the demand that parted her thighs to meet him. She heard his own voice. *Come with me, Anna.*

Confusion welled within her, wrapped in reality. Desire demanded. And above it all was the touch and taste and smell of a man who didn't even exist.

She put her hands to his chest, knowing it didn't matter how solid the muscle was beneath her palms. It was all an illusion. She pushed him away. Her breath came fast, her chest rising and falling as if after a struggle.

From the corner of her eye she saw him watching her. When she saw his hand rise, come toward her, she backed away. She wasn't angry at him. It was she who'd wanted it too much. Yet she couldn't risk one touch. She could only glance at him. Half-turned away, wrapping her arms about her, feeling the narrow width of her body, she envied him, the oblivion of his amnesia.

"What have I done, Anna?"

She wouldn't look at him. "Nothing." Sadness filled her as strongly as passion, only moments ago, had rendered her senseless.

"Tell me what's wrong." She felt the press of his voice.

What would be her answer? That K. C. Cowboy loved her, but Kent Landover was to wed another?

That she wasn't a countess, but a Clean Queen? That she had learned a long time ago that pretending things were something other than what they were only led to trouble and pain?

"Is there someone else?"

The tight rasp of her laugh surprised them both. "In a manner of speaking, yes."

"You've a boyfriend?"

She shook her head.

"A fiancé?"

Again she turned her head side to side.

"A lover?"

How could she explain? "It's complicated."

He turned her toward him. "Tell me."

She moved out of his hold. "There's no cowboy named K.C. There's no countess. There's only Kent Landover, and he most definitely isn't in love with a cleaning lady. You don't remember now, but one day, you will."

He grasped her arms. "Tell me what you see."

Surprised, she looked at him.

His hold tightened on her upper arms. "Tell me what you see."

She began at the wide-brimmed hat, brushed clean of specks, continued to the cotton shirt snapped tight across his chest, tucked into jeans washed soft and outlining the man's lean length. A silver-buckled belt wound around his narrow waist. His feet wore scuffed boots.

"I know what I see," she answered him.

"Now..." He pulled her up tight and pressed his

mouth to hers before she could protest. Then, even before she could begin to fight, he released her.

"Tell me what you feel."

She set her mouth into a grim line, ignoring the delicious tingle on her lips. She glared up at him.

He stepped back. "You think the problem is I don't remember."

"That's not the problem?" she challenged.

"There is a lot I don't remember. I don't remember how I made all this money they tell me is mine or why I built a big white box of a house or why I spent my days behind a desk in a room where the windows don't open. They tell me I did all that, and at this point, I've got no choice but to believe them, because I don't remember anything…except for one thing."

He reached for a stray strand of her hair, lifting it gently. "I remember you, Anna. You and me."

He tucked the hair behind her ear. "So the real problem is not that I've forgotten. The real problem is that you've forgotten."

He cupped her cheek. "But one day, you'll be able to remember—like I did. When you do, I'll be there." He pressed a kiss to her forehead, then touched his fingertips to the brim of his hat and walked away.

She watched him go. He was wrong, of course. She hadn't forgotten anything. All too well, she remembered a love between them could never last.

Chapter Five

The next morning Anna and Ronnie were going over the day's schedule when the front door banged against the wall. They looked up. In the rectangular frame stood Leon, panting. He aimed a finger at Anna.

"You!"

He slammed the door closed and came toward the desk. Ronnie wheeled back her chair and stood up, a five-foot-eleven-inch wall of well-toned muscle. "Mr. Skow, I'll give you the benefit of the doubt and assume this little display is only the result of too much pent-up sexual energy."

Anna stepped around Ronnie. Leon's face was moving past mottled red to crimson. "Goodness, Leon, what's wrong? Is Kent all right?"

"All right? He's never been better. At least, that's what he told me when he showed up at the office this morning looking like Hopalong Cassidy."

The skin along Leon's receding hairline deepened to purple. He began to pace.

"C'mon now, sit down, relax," Anna urged. "He doesn't look that bad."

Leon stopped midstride. His gaze narrowed on Anna. "You've seen him?"

She nodded. "When I got home last night, he was waiting for me on the step."

"You didn't tell me that," Ronnie interjected.

"What was he wearing?" Leon asked.

Anna shrugged. "Denim shirt, jeans, boots."

Leon eyed her. "That's it?"

"Hat. Belt with a big silver buckle."

Leon winced.

"Bandanna around his neck."

"This morning he switched to one of those string ties." Leon's voice was pained.

"What's so bad about that?" Ronnie wondered. "All cowboys dress like that."

Leon put a clenched fist to either temple. "He is *not* a cowboy!"

"Leon, Leon." Anna put her arm around the man's shoulders and guided him toward the velour chairs. "Sit down."

"I don't have time to sit," he protested even as he sank into the crimson cushions. "For all I know, the King of the Cowboys is out right now, trading company stock for livestock."

"But except for his wardrobe, he's okay?" Anna asked once more.

Leon looked at her, his answer expressed in his raised eyebrows.

"Relatively speaking?" she added.

Before Leon could answer, a voice like a calm summer wind came from the back of the room.

"Such commotion for civilized people," Maureen scolded, but her voice was pleasant. She came forward, hands entwined and resting on the shelf of her bosom. She smiled at Leon.

"Hello."

"Mom, this is Leon Skow," Anna introduced. "Kent's business associate. Leon," she said as the man rose from the chair, "this is my mother."

"Maureen Delaney," Anna's mother said, extending her hand. "Please sit down." She arranged herself into the chair next to Leon. "Would you like a cup of peppermint tea?"

"Peppermint tea?" Leon looked from one woman to the other. He threw his hands up as he sank back into the deep red cushions. "Peppermint tea?"

Maureen's kind smile didn't alter. "It's lovely with cream and sugar."

Leon gave her a long look. His hands rose once more. "Why not?"

Maureen's smile became pleased. "Is the pot on?" she said to her daughter.

Anna walked to the square cart in the corner where two electric pots were plugged in. One was filled with coffee, the other with hot water. She opened the tin box of tea, releasing scents, sharp and crisp as spring.

"How is our K.C.?" she heard her mother ask.

Anna glanced over her shoulder. Leon was shaking his head.

"He's not hurt, is he?" Maureen's concern echoed her daughter's earlier fear.

"No."

Anna poured hot water.

"He's unhappy, then?"

There was a pause. "I wouldn't say that."

"He's not hurt, and he's not unhappy," Anna heard her mother summarize. She looked over her shoulder and saw her mother was smiling a small smile.

"But there's a problem?" Maureen reached over and patted Leon's hand.

Leon nodded. His features contorted. "He's bought a ranch."

The cup of tea slid from Anna's hand, splashed across the floor. She felt hot drops hit her legs. She didn't move.

Maureen got up and, stepping around the puddle, went to her daughter. "He's bought a ranch," her mother repeated softly.

"Cool!" Ronnie said.

"Quite cool," Maureen agreed, taking the spoon and napkin from her daughter's still hand. She looked into Anna's eyes.

Leon stood. "Just like that." He snapped his fingers. "Put his house on the market this morning—"

"That joint *LA Magazine* did the spread on last summer?" Ronnie interrupted. She let out a low whistle. "That'll fetch some chicken feed."

"Ronnie," Maureen said as she guided Anna toward a chair, "be my salvation and bring out the roll of paper towels under the bathroom sink."

"He's also broken off his engagement with Hilary," Leon announced.

Anna and her mother both stopped. Ronnie, on her way to the back, turned around.

"Hilary realizes it's only temporary. She knows everything will be back to normal as soon as Kent's memory comes back. She's just praying it'll be before three-fourths of Beverly Hills shows up in a few weeks for the wedding of the year."

Anna sank into the chair.

Leon looked down at her with a laser-beam gaze. "He didn't tell you anything about all of this when you saw him last night?"

She shook her head.

He looked at her a moment longer, then he began to pace again, his words as quick as his steps. "We were making progress yesterday. He went to the hospital for some tests in the morning. Hilary brought him into the office after lunch—"

"He went back to work yesterday?" Maureen asked. "Less than a day after his accident?"

Leon paused. "Are you kidding me? If he'd been his old self when he woke up from the crash, he would've made the ambulance bring him to the office instead of the hospital."

Leon took two steps, stopped again, looked at the ladies. "*All work, no play.* That's how Kent Landover got where he is today."

Maureen's small smile returned. "I would have to agree with you there, Mr. Skow."

"Things were looking good yesterday." Leon circled. "He did spend an hour trying to find a vendor to put beef jerky in the machines in the employees' cafeteria. And one salesman did mention Kent had asked him if he'd like to see a rope trick.''

Maureen's smile widened.

"But it was his first day back. He has amnesia.'' Leon raised his hands in appeal. "At least he was wearing Burberry."

His hands fell. "Then this morning he comes in, all boots and silver buckles, straddles my office chair and announces he'd be 'saddlin' up' in a few days."

Leon's gaze closed in on Anna. "He and his countess."

She stared back at him. Her skin felt tight, pulling at her features, her lips pursing to protest.

"This is all your fault," Leon said.

"Wait a minute, bub." Ronnie, wiping up the tea, started to rise, a wad of paper towel in one fist.

Leon's impaling stare stayed on Anna. "He did it all for you."

Maureen nodded in serene agreement. "Of course he did. He loves her."

"Mama!" Anna's voice came.

Her mother placed her hand on her shoulder. "She loves him, too."

"Is that so?" Leon looked at Anna.

Anna's mother patted her shoulder. "Only, the Irish in her hasn't admitted it yet." Her mother winked at her. "But it will, and when it does, my Anna will be as happy as our K.C."

"Really?" The word came out of Leon slow and sarcastic. He looked at Anna and her mother. "You think when Kent's memory returns, and he finds out his main assets are cow chips instead of computer chips, he's going to be happy?''

His voice rose as he stepped toward them. ''You're telling me when Kent recovers and finds his company in ruins, his home sold and his bride-to-be suing him for breach of contract, he's going to be filled with ecstasy?''

''Was he happy before?'' Maureen asked as she went to the cart to make a new cup of tea.

''Before what?'' Exasperation clipped Leon's words.

Maureen dunked the tea bag up and down. ''Before the accident?''

''Was he happy before the accident? I don't know. I never asked him.'' Leon rubbed at his receding hairline. ''We came to work, we made money. We moved up, we got bigger, we made more money. What else is there?''

Maureen turned and smiled. ''Oh, Mr. Skow,'' she murmured, coming toward him with his tea.

He waved his hand, dismissing her soft utterances. ''Don't start selling me that New Age meaning-of-life nonsense. I get enough of that crap just walking through LAX.'' He took the tea, took a large swallow, grimaced. ''Right now I need more than platitudes and peppermint tea parties.''

Maureen's hands folded prayerlike and rested against her bosom. ''What can we do to help?''

Leon's gaze went to Anna.

She responded with an artificial laugh. ''Don't look

at me that way. I'm the source of all this trouble, remember?''

Leon nodded. ''You are part of the problem. You may also be part of the solution.''

''In what way?'' Anna's mother asked.

''Kent told me he's not going up to the ranch until Anna goes with him, so—''

''You can stop right there.'' Anna held up a halting hand. ''You're worried Kent Landover is going to walk in here, snap his fingers and I'll run away with him to some second-chance ranch?''

Before Leon could reply, Anna's mother said in her soothing voice, ''Honey, it's an honest mistake on Mr. Skow's part. K.C. is very charming. He's also handsome, hardworking and head over heels about you.''

''And I bet he looks some fine in a pair of chaps,'' Ronnie added.

Anna gave both women long-suffering looks. She turned back to Leon. ''You thought I'd drop everything and run off with a man who, as soon as all that fresh air hits him, will probably come to his senses and ask me, 'Who the hell are you?'''

''Actually…'' Leon took another swallow of tea, then set the cup down on Ronnie's desk. He looked Anna straight in the eye. ''I was hoping that's exactly what you'd do.''

''What?'' Anna felt her eyes widen, her brows rise. She glanced at her mother. Maureen didn't dare smile, but her palms pressed together in an expression of pleasure.

Anna looked back at Leon. "Obviously Kent isn't the only one who has temporarily set aside his sanity."

"Hear me out." Leon's voice switched into persuasive mode. "In less than forty-eight hours, Kent has, one—" Leon's pointed finger arced upward like a conductor's baton "—wandered about L.A. in foam rubber slippers."

The hand swooped down. "Two, declared his undying devotion to an ad campaign—"

"Mr. Skow," Maureen began, but Anna laid a hand on her mother's forearm.

The mother looked down at her daughter. She stayed silent.

"Three, canceled his wedding to Hilary because he doesn't love her—a fact that Hilary will tell you herself didn't stop him from proposing to her in the first place. Four—" the hand made a complete sweep "—spent the better part of his work day teaching the secretarial pool 'The Honky Tonk Twist.'"

"He sounds like a true menace to society," Ronnie noted.

"Finally, five…" Both hands rose, readying for the grand finale. "He's out there somewhere, right now, swaggering the streets of L.A. in a Stetson and spurs." Leon's raised hands appealed to Anna. "It's only a matter of time before someone notices."

"Is it that bad?" Anna attempted to soothe. "So he's out there somewhere dressed a little differently? We're in L.A. Eccentricity isn't a rare commodity."

Leon shook his head. "I'm not talking eccentricity.

In two days Kent Landover has undergone a complete transformation. He's not the same man."

"That's bad?" Anna's mother wondered.

Leon looked at her. "It's not good. For Landover Tech, it can be downright disastrous. One little whiff something is not quite right, and our competitors will be on us like hounds to the hunt. On top of that, our proposed Japanese partners have us under a magnifying glass, looking for any potential weaknesses before the deal is done that would make Landover Tech the biggest PC supplier in the world. Believe me, our enemies and even our allies are right outside our door, waiting for us to screw up. It's not a prime time for the company president to decide to 'git along with the dogies.' "

"I understand your concern," Anna sympathized, "but you said yourself, Kent's memory should return shortly, and everything will be back to normal."

"What if it's not?" Leon challenged. "One howdy-doody to the wrong person, and it could be happy trails to Landover Tech. I'm not willing to take that risk. This ranch might be a blessing in disguise. At least Kent would be out of the L.A. limelight until he's his old self again."

Leon looked at Anna. "But he won't go until you do."

She stood up. "That's impossible."

"On the contrary, it's very possible. We've got the ranch, the cowboy...now all we need is the countess." Up came the finger baton once more. It pointed at Anna. "You."

She looked around the semicircle of others waiting for her answer. "I'm not a countess," she told them, her voice louder than she'd anticipated. "I'm not a countess."

She saw disappointment on their faces. "Are you all crazy, too? A man bumps his head, says he's a cowboy, swears I'm a countess, and you all are expecting me to pack my bags and run off with him to play *Little House on the Prairie?* Something's not quite right with this picture."

"The idea has more merit than you realize," Anna's mother said in her composed voice. "By indulging a person's remote memory, there's a significant chance recent memory will be stimulated."

Anna looked at her mother, then at Leon. "She just made that up."

"Actually, the doctors at UCLA said something similar," Leon said. "Studies of amnesia cases show a direct correlation between the emphasis on remote memory and the subsequent swift return of recent memory."

Anna looked at her mother.

"I heard it on *General Hospital,*" her mother said.

Anna looked at her mother a moment longer before addressing Leon. "So, by sending Kent to the ranch, not only is he out of sight, but his memory is stimulated?"

Leon rubbed his hands together. "Perfect plan, huh?"

"What if Kent's memory doesn't come back before the wedding?"

"The wedding is the least of our problems. The Sushima people are arriving next week, and, believe me, eight hundred special-order crystal favors are nothing compared to losing this deal. We've been working on this partnership for over two years now. Next week they're coming to California to give us a final inspection. They'll be expecting one of the computer industry's cutting-edge CEOs, not some John Wayne wannabe."

"And if Kent's memory hasn't come back by then?" Anna asked.

"Don't even say it." Leon paced in a straight line. "If worse comes to worst, I'll stall, I'll postpone. I'll employ creative crisis-management tactics. Fingers crossed, Kent's memory will have returned in toto, but if not, I'd rather have him up at the ranch than two-stepping all over L.A."

"It sounds like you've got everything figured out," Anna noted.

"He certainly does," her mother agreed.

"So…" Leon rubbed his hands together once more. "We're all agreed—"

"Leon, I sympathize—"

"No, not the 'I sympathize' speech," he interrupted. "You have to go. You're the only one."

"I'm not going," Anna said.

Leon stared at her.

"I'm not going," she repeated quietly.

Leon looked in appeal to her mother.

"I'm afraid that's it, Mr. Skow. My daughter's as stubborn as she is beautiful."

Leon looked back at Anna. "Give me a reason. One good reason."

She looked at the man before her. His stance was wide legged, the set of his mouth fierce, but his eyes were earnest in appeal. The phone rang. She heard Ronnie answer it, heard her Clean Queen spiel.

She could claim she couldn't leave the business, so new and vulnerable. It would be only half a lie. She was needed now by the Clean Queens in these critical first weeks.

Leon had also listened to Ronnie's patter, a smile starting at the hard corners of his mouth, and his eyes changed from appeal to idea.

"Is it the business?" he asked. "This is a new venture, isn't it? You're afraid to leave it? Is that the problem?"

She was tempted to agree and be done with the entire conversation. But she knew in her heart it wouldn't be the truth. She did have high hopes for the business, but the fact was, at the moment all those hopes were being met.

"Nonsense," Maureen answered for her. "For its first month of operation, the business is doing well. And if it didn't, we'd survive. We have in the past, and we will again. I'm not worried. There's always somebody out there making a mess and looking for someone else to clean it up."

Ronnie hung up the phone. "Possible new client wants an estimate."

Maureen smiled at her daughter and Leon. "Case closed."

Leon gazed at Anna once more, waiting for her answer. Her mother's gaze was on her, too, her eyes saying, *Listen to your heart, darling.*

She was listening to her heart. That was the problem. She could hear its call, could feel its need. She couldn't chance days alone with Kent; she couldn't risk nights, the darkness falling like an intimate drape, the land merging with the sky, and all other things unreal. Except desire.

Leon watched, waiting for her answer. Ronnie was silent at her desk. Anna's mother smiled as if to give her daughter strength. Her gaze hoped for happiness.

Anna looked from her mother to Leon. "I can't go" was all she said. She said nothing more.

THE DAY PASSED without questions, and night brought the promise of repose. But sleep didn't come easily to Anna in these hours. If she had been sleeping when she first heard the music, she'd have thought she dreamed it. But she was awake when the first chords came in through the window opened to the night. She listened, lying in the single bed in the room above the storefront, the streetlight drawing silver shadows on the inside of her closed lids.

The song came. It was not as smooth as a CD track from a moving car or as strong as the beat of a boom box hoisted on a passing shoulder. It came, no more than a lone voice singing in the night's dark. It came. A love song.

She'd never minded the night noises from the street. It was why she'd chosen the front room, leaving the back bedroom to her mother. On the contrary, she found the night noises comforting. It was the silence, calling forth thoughts and desires, that she feared.

The song ended, then began again in the same tenor. It was a pleasant voice, untrained and a little flat, a typical voice with a typical need to lift in song. She listened, lulled now by the single, simple chords of a harmonica. She listened, hearing the words sung in a slow rolling call, words telling of mountains and roads, of hearts and hope and whiskey, of moonlight and ladies.

She might have even been humming along when she heard the horse's whinny. Her eyes opened. The rest of her body lay still. The silver shadows had left her lids and were now dancing on the walls.

Even as she called herself a fool, she lay alert. The song kept on, the harmonica wailed. A horse whinnied.

Anna sat straight up this time and looked to the screen that filtered the night's creatures. The moon was solid in the sky. In boxer shorts and a tank top, she tiptoed to the window, knelt by its side and peeked from a corner. On the sidewalk below, a man sat atop a horse. His face, beneath the wide brim of his hat, turned to her window. His voice lifted. His love became music.

"Kent!" Her hushed appeal sailed through the screen, was not heard. Below, the refrain began.

"Kent!" she called a little louder, showing more

of herself at the window. He saw her. The song stopped.

"What are you doing?"

He smiled up at her. "I'm singing."

"I can see that. Why?"

His smile widened. The streetlight gilded his features.

"Because I love you."

As the words reached her ears, her heart, she heard a voice behind her, speaking her name.

She spun around. Her mother, soft in the folds of a long gown, stood in the doorway.

She stepped into the room. "Is everything all right?"

"No, unless you like country music."

Her mother came to the window where Anna knelt, and looked out. She chuckled, the laugh tender.

"Good evening, K.C."

"Evenin' to you, ma'am."

"Sheesh!" Anna exclaimed.

"Nice night out." Anna's mother continued the conversation.

"Yes, it is," Kent agreed.

"You got yourself a horse."

"Never walk when you can ride, ma'am."

Her mother's tender laugh answered.

"You're not helping this situation," Anna appealed.

Her mother looked back from the window. "Honey, he was serenading you. That's so sweet."

"You say sweet." Anna stood up, walked to the

brass-plated coatrack in the corner. She lifted a gold kimono from its hook and wrapped it around her. "Others say psychotic." She pulled the robe's sash tight around her waist.

"What do you say, dear?"

Anna looked at her mother, her figure soft in the night's backlight. "I'd say there's a fine line."

Her mother's gentle laugh fell upon Anna and followed her as she padded barefoot down the stairs. The streetlight grayed the empty office. Framed in the front windows, colored unreal by the moon's glaze, was a cowboy on a horse.

She crossed the room and opened the door. The horse swung its head toward her. One rheumy eye gazed at her without interest. A blaze once white along the long length of the animal's face had yellowed. A tuft of forelock along the brow was thin and brittle. In the center of its sagging back sat Kent, a harmonica in his hand, a Stetson on his head, a wide smile across his face. Anna didn't know whether to laugh or cry. For a moment she feared she'd do both.

The horse puffed air through its nostrils once in a soft snort, then lowered its head back to a late-night snack of front lawn.

"Evenin', Anna." Kent touched the beige brim of his hat.

She stared back at him. "There must be an ordinance against this sort of thing inside the city limits."

He laughed, a rich baritone sent into the sheen of the night. Swinging a leg over that broad, swayed back, he dismounted. The horse didn't miss a chew.

Kent bent down to it as he passed and, patting the long, flat plane of its neck, whispered a secret in its ear.

Still smiling, he came to Anna. Admiration was in his gaze. "Royal robes." He nodded his pleasure.

She looked down at the colorful kimono. Her lips pulled together to protest.

"You're beautiful," he said.

Her breath caught. Words fell away. She looked up at him, his features shaded, drawing her. A weave of moonlight blurred the night's boundaries. Light became dark; dark became light. A cleaning girl became a countess. A corporate CEO became a cowboy.

Chapter Six

She backed away, one hand flitting about behind her, reaching for something to hold on to. She felt only the nothing of the night air. The horse paused. Rolling an eye, he watched her. Anna stopped her retreat.

Head hardly raised, the horse gave a slow shake. A flat, wet snort blew from his nostrils.

"Easy, big daddy." Kent stroked the animal's slanted neck. He winked at Anna. "White Lightning's a bit skittish, but he's cut proud is all. Underneath, this pony's all heart."

"White Lightning?" Anna looked at the animal chewing in unrelenting rhythm. Bits of grass fluttered from his lower lip.

"White Lightning?" she said again.

Kent ran a hand across a grayed, full flank. "A true outlaw."

Anna looked at the horse gumming the grass. "When you were little, you had a horse." She stepped toward the animal. She looked at Kent. "Your parents made you call him Sir Goodwood."

Her fingers reached hesitantly toward the animal.

She touched the forehead where the once-white streak began. "But we always called him White Lightning."

She looked at Kent. "This isn't...?"

He nodded. His hand, too, stroked the horse.

"No, it couldn't—"

He smiled. "Why not?"

She looked at the horse's lowered head. Slowly she circled, following the spine's deep dip, the fleshy curve of spreading flanks. Her gentle hand never left the horse. She came back to the head, laid her own head against a dappled shoulder. Beneath her cheek was a brush of warmth, like a dream begun.

She lifted her head. "But your father had him sold. We went to the stall one afternoon, and he was gone." She looked past Kent. "Like that." Her hand leveled the air. "As if he never was."

"You cried," Kent said.

Her gaze came back to him, her voice mild. "So did you."

"I loved him."

She lowered her head once more, her voice muffled. "I loved him, too."

"My father found us crying."

Coleman Landover. Anna had seen him only three times in the four years she'd lived on the Landover estate. A cold, long-jawed man used to giving orders and having them followed. She'd been terrified of him. As had his son.

"He sent you away," Kent said. "He called me a child."

She raised her head. She saw a six-year-old's defiance in the squaring of his shoulders.

"You were a child. We both were."

She looked down to their two hands tangled across the horse's broad back, not sure who had reached for the other first.

"He told me to be a man."

There was a moment's silence. Then Kent said, "I only wanted White Lightning."

"You were a child. No one listens to a child. How can a child know what's best? How can a child know what he wants?"

Kent looked her in the eye. "I wanted White Lightning."

She smiled softly. "Now you have him."

"I found out later he'd been sold to a riding school outside the city. It was an easy life for him, easier than most. Still, it shouldn't have happened. I should've done something."

"You were a child," she told him again.

He ran his free hand down the horse's long neck. "But now I'm not."

She looked at him. For a moment she almost believed, believed all they had to do was slip a foot into the stirrup, swing a leg up and across and mount this old gelding. Then, with no more than a tug of the reins, Kent and she, sitting thigh-to-thigh, her arms wrapped around his waist, holding on tight, would ride off into their childhood past. For a moment, a lovely moment, she almost believed.

"He made you leave, too, didn't he?"

The dream ended at the sound of his voice. She slid her hand from his hold.

"You and your mother? He made you both leave."

She modeled her features into blandness, hiding the sharp twist of humiliation which, even after all these years, struck. "Yes."

"It was my fault."

"No. It was no one's fault. It was a misunderstanding."

He spoke as if he didn't hear her. "It was my fault. I loved you. He took away everything I loved. After that I did everything he said, became everything he wanted, so he wouldn't take away anything else I loved." His eyes, the color of nightshade, looked past her. "But it was too late. Everything I loved was already gone."

She wanted to soothe his pain, her pain. "I would've stayed if I could."

He looked at her, and she knew he saw yesterday, their early happiness, the ease and simplicity of their world then.

"Stay now," he said.

Longing like a blocked breath filled her. "It's not that simple." She made her voice light. "Not as simple as rescuing White Lightning and riding him here."

He shook his head, the overhead light stirring the shadows on his face. "You city gals are the cutest. You think I just saddled up and trotted a horse down the interstate?"

"No, but—" She felt foolish. Then she remem-

bered she wasn't the one who had dressed like Little
Joe Cartwright, sat on a horse on an L.A. street and
sung country love songs at three in the morning.

"All I see is a horse and you."

He chuckled again, then pointed to where the main
thoroughfare met this side street. "The truck and
trailer are parked a few blocks over. This dead end
street is too narrow to turn around in."

"Of course," she said. She looked at him—a big-
time businessman dressed pure cowboy, serenading
the stars in the middle of the night...and making perfect sense. How did he do that—make the ridiculous
seem reasonable? How did he make her doubt everything she knew? How did he make her believe, for
even a brief moment, he was a cowboy...she was a
countess?

"I promised myself and Lightning, one day I'd buy
my own spread, a little piece of hog heaven. So that's
what I did—I bought a ranch. Nothing fancy, a square
of land up north, near the border. We'll call it—"

"The Rocking Horse Ranch." Looking straight
into his eyes, she said it before she realized it.

He smiled. "You remember."

She looked away, smoothed the horse's age-
dappled coat. She'd never forgotten.

He touched her hand. "You remember because I
promised you, too."

Her hand slipped away, moved farther down the
horse's neck.

"I've got my horse, my ranch."

He was quiet until she looked at him. "I need you."

She looked at him, across the divide of the horse's back. She moved back a step, but her eyes stayed on him.

He'd been a beautiful boy; he'd become a handsome man. In tailored three-piece suits and tight-knotted silk ties, he'd been compelling. Now he wore a cotton shirt, sleeves rolled up, revealing strong forearms. A silver-buckled belt cinched tight his jeans. His boots were curtained with a stacked drag of denim. His wide-brimmed hat was pulled low, adding shadows to the strong lines of his face. And *compelling* didn't even begin the description. He was so beautiful, so devastating, she couldn't find a word for the image before her. Only a feeling. Desire came to her—hot, low, painful. She looked away, knowing already it was too late. She'd been branded.

When her breath came back full, she looked once more at this cowboy and his mount.

"We need to talk."

She took his hand and led him to the front step. They sat down, side by side, a splay of light silhouetting their figures. The horse chewed. Anna looked out into the night.

She was hesitant to begin. "It's okay not to tie up Lightning, isn't it?" she teased for time. "He's not going to terrorize the neighborhood or anything?"

From the corner of her eye she watched Kent's smile come. "Fertilize, maybe. Terrorize, no."

She smiled, too. They sat there a moment in silence, smiling, the wash of the night's lights on them.

"Kent—"

"Call me K.C., please, Anna."

She turned to him. The moonlight highlighted his handsomeness, and she made a mental image of this moment—the negative light of the night, the reverse logic of love.

She forced her voice soft, its tone quiet. Inside, she felt only its waver. "We became friends a long time ago. When we were very young. No more than children."

He smiled.

"There was a huge house. You lived there."

He looked at her. "You lived there."

"There was a small cottage in the back. I lived there. Do you remember?"

"I remember you."

"Nothing else?" she asked.

He tilted his head and took her breath away. "It's enough."

She had to turn from him then or be forever lost in a world not real—except for Kent...and once, a long time ago, for her, too. She met Lightning's watery stare, his eyes liquid, all tears.

She looked up, not to the stars or the moon, but to the blackness. Still, there was no absolute. Only shades darker or lighter.

"Kent—"

"K.C."

When he said the name so soft, so low, she had to

turn to him. With the night's permission, she touched the side of his face. For so long she'd loved a man who'd existed only in memory, in imaginings. Many times she'd called herself a fool for loving someone found only in paper or projected image. She'd told herself it wasn't real. She'd tried to love another. She'd failed.

Now the only man she'd ever loved was here, beside her, the pulse in her wrist aligned with the pulse in his throat. And still he didn't exist.

Her hand fell. She removed the tenderness in her voice.

"Kent, we were children then. We were very young. We played together on the grounds, in the big house, in the cottage. We pretended. We made an imaginary world—a world that wasn't real. Do you understand?"

She looked at him. "It was a world that didn't exist except for you and me. Do you understand?"

He nodded. She knew he didn't understand.

"Look at the building behind me."

He looked at wide window storefronts.

"Does that look like the home of a countess? I clean other people's houses for a living. Houses much larger and fancier. Is that the work of a countess?"

He looked back at her. "I know a title doesn't always guarantee more than an impressive signature or maybe a drafty castle or two. Many family fortunes are lost through bad investments or poor management. It's nothing to be ashamed about."

"I'm not—"

She tried once more to tell him she wasn't a countess, but he wouldn't let her finish. "Of course, you're not ashamed. There's no shame in a hard day's work and earning an honest living. On the contrary, I'm downright proud of you."

She could only stare at his admiring expression. She raised her hands, squaring her palms as if to present her words in a neat little box. "Listen to me." She heard the keen of desperation in her voice. "What you're remembering, what you think is real, is actually only an imaginary world created by two children."

He watched her, the brim of his hat level with his brow. She looked down. Her hands fell, smoothed the golden silk along her lap.

"Much time has passed since then. We were separated. We grew up, became what we are. That world you remember is no more, is gone forever. That world never was." She didn't know where the shake in her voice came from. She only knew she despised it.

"It's gone," she made herself say again. "Except you were hurt, and you can't remember. But soon you will."

His fingertips touched her chin, tilted her face toward him. Still, she couldn't meet his eyes. She saw the pearl snaps along his shirtfront, shining softly near his heart.

"It's not gone, Anna. It's right here." He took her hand, pressing the palm to the pearl circles and the beat of his heart beneath. "I'm right here before you, beside you. I'm real. You're real."

He took her hand, held it in both his own. "Except you were hurt, and you can't remember."

Her head came up, her gaze to his as she heard her own words repeated.

"But soon you will."

She heard his voice, heard the irrational become reasonable, the absurd make sense. She felt her body moving toward him, a sole star being pulled into another's orbit, held fast by fate.

"No." She pulled her palm away from his pulse. Her hand slapped against the hard step. Lightning looked up, stopped chewing.

Words weren't going to work, she realized. Logic and reason were no longer enough. She rubbed her forehead, closed her eyes, longing for crisp daylight. There was only more darkness. She opened her eyes, saw Kent's hand hovering above her silk-covered shoulder.

"I've upset you. That isn't why I came." His hand hung in the air, helpless.

"Please go," she said.

Stay, she thought. She closed her eyes to the world. *Stay,* she prayed, seeing her arms circling his neck, bringing him close, her mouth to his ear, summoning him softly. *Stay.*

She forced her eyes open, seeing what was, knowing only what could be. She'd loved him always; he loved her now. It didn't matter. One blink, one bump, and it'd be over. His memory would return. Reason would resume. Would he love her then? She'd be lucky if he recognized her. No, like the man before her, this love didn't exist, except for fanciful imaginings and damaged memories. In the end, he would marry Hilary. And she would have her heart broken.

"You want me to go, Anna? Is that what you want?"

Frustration filled her throat, letting no more useless words free. She could only nod.

"I'll go now because you ask me, but I'll come back."

It was a given, not a possibility. His world was all black and white. There was no gray; no ifs or buts.

She felt his hand pass across her crown, the lightest touch of his lips on her hair. "One day I'll stay, one day when you realize I never really left. Good night, Anna. Sweet dreams."

She watched him walk to his horse, rubbing the animal's coat as he passed. The horse's head rose. Kent slipped one foot into a stirrup and mounted. He gathered the reins in one hand. With his other, he touched the brim of his hat and nodded to Anna. Lightning gave her one last long look. Then the horse turned, responding to Kent's easy pull on the reins. The horse ambled off, guided to the soft shoulder of the road between the hard surfaces of the street and the sidewalk. Kent sat tall, proud, his body moving with the animal's easy saunter. The rider and horse move off into the tilted shadows. She watched until she saw them no more. Then she sat, waiting for daylight.

SHE DOZED into a dreamless sleep, waking hours later, stiff from the step's hard bed. Dawn had long come. Past the closed door behind her, a phone was ringing, ringing, ringing. She stood up too quickly. The world circled black. She grabbed the doorknob and held on. The world cleared. She turned the knob and went inside. The clock over Ronnie's desk told her office hours didn't begin for another two hours. She picked up the phone.

"The Clean Queens," she began automatically. "We'll give your castle—"

"Is he with you?" Leon's voice erupted across the wire.

Reality turned upside down again. She closed her eyes, took a breath, forcing the world to right itself once more.

"Is he?" Leon demanded.

"No."

"Then where is he?"

Sudden fear for Kent's well-being filled her. She reminded herself panic was Leon's natural state. She leaned against the desk edge, pushing back her apprehension.

"He's home," she stated, as if spoken conviction alone could make it true. Still her fear swelled.

"I've been calling for over a hour. He doesn't answer."

She sat down. The fear rose up. "He was here—"

Leon swore. "When?"

"In the middle of the night. About three o'clock." The fear she didn't want to feel grew.

"Freakin' three in the morning? What the hell was he doing at three in the morning at your place?"

"Singing," she said. *He's okay, he's okay*, repeated inside her.

"What the hell...?"

"He was singing in the street. I guess you'd say he was serenading me."

"Serenading you? In the street?" Leon moaned. "He's ready for the white wagons."

"The man sang a song." She tried to calm Leon...and her own beating heart. "I wouldn't call that deranged behavior. If you think about it, it's actually sort of sweet. My mother was completely charmed."

"Great. We've got a completely charming but crazy cowboy roaming the city. What time did he leave?"

"It must have been around four."

"Did he say where he was going?"

"Where else would he go at that time but home? I'm sure if you went there right now, you'd find him in a deep sleep. He probably never even heard the phone."

"What direction did he go when he drove away?"

"West, but he wasn't—"

"West. Of course, west—would it be any other direction for our rootin'-tootin' cowboy? Not that it matters. He could be anywhere by now."

"Leon—"

"What?"

"He wasn't in a car when he left. He was—"

"Walking? Why didn't you say so? Walking is good. Walking is slow, takes time."

"He wasn't walking."

"He called a cab?"

"No."

"A bus?" Leon's questions came rapid-fire.

"No."

"What, then? How'd he leave your place?"

"He rode away on a horse." She braced herself for Leon's reaction.

There was silence. It scared Anna more than the string of sailor's curses she'd expected.

"Leon? Are you still with me?"

"A horse," he repeated quietly.

Dry laughter began.

"Are you okay, Leon?"

"A horse. Of course." The laughter was a little louder. "Every cowboy has to have a horse. Did he have a wagon, too?"

"No, just a harmonica."

The phone line seemed to swell with Leon's laughter. Anna waited, listening for the on-the-edge rumble to end.

"Well, then, our problem is solved. All we have to do is look for a singing, harp-playing cowboy riding a horse around the streets of L.A. That should be no problem at all."

"He wasn't going to ride the horse through the city."

"No? What was he going to do? Have it airlifted?"

"He had a trailer and a truck."

"Of course, of course. He'd have a truck and a trailer. I'll bet the truck was a Chevy? Did you get the license plate?"

"No."

"Why not?"

"For Pete's sake, Leon, he's a grown man."

"A grown man dressed like a bit player in a spaghetti Western. A grown man riding horseback in L.A. in the middle of the night, singing. He's crazy."

"Charming," she insisted.

Leon sighed. "What color was the truck? The trailer? Was the truck a Chevy?"

"I don't know. He'd parked a few streets over."

"Of course. Why pull up in a pickup when you can trot in on horseback? Definitely more dramatic."

"My street's a dead end. Kent said it was too narrow to turn the vehicles around, so he parked on the main street."

"Makes perfect sense. Everything makes perfect sense." Leon's voice was a blend of exasperation and frustration.

"This animal was special to him. He had him a long time ago, when he was a child, no more than five. His father sold him when Kent was seven. We called him White Lightning."

"We?"

"My mother and I were living on the Landover estate then. His father sold Lightning about a month before we left."

"And this is the same horse?"

"Yes."

"How do you know?"

How did she know? "He said so."

"He said so?" She didn't need Leon's sarcasm to tell her how gullible she'd been.

"It looked like him," she attempted to defend herself.

"It looked like him?" The exasperation increased in Leon's voice. "First off, few horses live that long. Secondly, even if by some miracle it was the same horse, more likely than not it wouldn't even look the same."

"It was smaller and whiter the last time I saw it."

"Let me get this straight. In the middle of the night Kent shows up beneath your window on a horse he claims is the same horse he owned about twenty-five years ago, a horse that probably went to the glue factory when the old man sold him."

"Your sensitivity knows no bounds, Leon."

"He sings you a little ditty, then rides off into the night?"

"That's right." It had been so real. Now it was only ridiculous.

"I've one more question for you. Why didn't you call someone?"

"Who'd you want me to call—the police?"

"Me!"

When she put the phone back to her ear, Leon was saying, "I want you to call me."

The rhythm of his speech and breath was swift, and she knew his steps followed suit back and forth across the room. "Perhaps you're right. Perhaps I should've called you, but, well, Kent and I sat and talked, and he seemed so calm, so tranquil, so sure of himself..." She paused, trying to find the words to explain. "I know it sounds strange, but when he talks to you, it's almost as if he's the one making sense, and the rest of the world is all wrong."

"What'd you do? Tell him that? You didn't tell him that, did you?" Leon was definitely pacing.

"I've done nothing to encourage Kent's behavior." She allowed the anger into her voice. "I'm trying to help him."

"If you wanted to help him, you'd go up with him to that godforsaken ranch of his until he regains his memory."

She walked over to the wide front windows, looking out to where Kent had ridden off last night. "I can't do that."

"Why not?"

Because she was afraid—afraid of her feelings, afraid of getting hurt. As last night had shown her, she wasn't safe.

"I'm certain if you try his house again, you'll find him." She evaded Leon's question.

"At the moment I can't be certain about anything concerning Kent Landover," his partner said.

He gave her his phone numbers—home, office, cellular, beeper—and made her promise twice to call him immediately if she saw Kent. She gave him her numbers and made him promise the same thing.

She hung up and stood at the front windows, looking out. Why had she accepted the horse was White

Lightning? Why had she let Kent ride off into the night as if it were the most natural thing in the world? In the morning's light she saw how absurd his actions were, how irrational his reality had become, how dangerous his behavior could be. Leon could see it. The media, the public, anyone who caught a glimpse of the present Kent Landover would see it. It would be clear to anyone who came into contact with Kent that he was acting oddly, his reasoning based more on soul and spirit than sense. Everyone could see that.

Everyone but her.

Why?

The warmth of the sun had begun, but the glass was still cool as she leaned her forehead to it. Why couldn't she see what was so obvious?

Because she was beginning to believe in him.

Her eyes were open when the answer came.

Chapter Seven

She stepped back from the touch of light and glass. She'd go upstairs, get cleaned up, dressed. Begin the day. End the night.

She turned and saw herself in the poster hung on the wall beside Ronnie's desk. It was a shot from the commercial. One leg kicked high. A bright pink feather duster flaunted. Her crown had slipped to a jaunty slant. She was too thin, as awkward as an adolescent, all elbows and knees and angles. She was smiling, openmouthed, the sliver of space between her two front teeth visible. Then there was that hair— masses and masses of a hennaed hurly-burly, daring gel or spray or any man-made taming device yet devised.

She shook her head, and the wayward weight of that hair shifted along her scalp. "Some countess," she said to the poster as she passed.

By the time she'd come back downstairs, laced her sneakers and started out on her daily morning walk-run, she'd almost convinced herself everything was fine. The smog was little, and the clouds hung close.

Everything would be okay, she'd decided. Then she turned the corner and saw the truck and trailer shining silver midblock.

He's sleeping inside the truck, she told herself, even as she went closer and saw the trailer was empty. *Please let him be inside the cab sleeping.* Her thoughts altered into prayer.

She peered into the front of the truck. The cab was empty. She stepped back and, her hand shielding her forehead, looked up and down the street as if sheer expectation would produce Kent astride an ambling Lightning.

She ran all the way back to her building. There was no answer at any of the numbers Leon had given her. She left a message on his beeper.

He called her back instantly.

"I'm at his house," he said. "He's here, and he's hurt."

She heard the words and dropped the phone. She ran upstairs, into the small parlor, cozy with hand-crocheted doilies and the smell of lemon oil. Her mother, a terry robe belted and bowed around her ample waist, stood in the doorway dividing the living room from the narrow kitchen.

"What's wrong?"

Anna waved aside her question. "Keys, keys," she muttered, dumping her too-big purse on the corduroy couch and pawing through the spill.

"Anna." Her mother covered her scrambling hands, stilling them. She lifted the right one where a plastic bracelet coiled around her wrist. Keys hung from the elastic circle.

"What is it?" her mother asked once more.

"Kent. He's hurt" was all she said as she ran out of the room.

She got on the Five North, cursing L.A.'s morning rush-hour traffic. Her curses circled to Kent. What kind of person rides a horse through the streets of L.A. in the middle of the night?

A cowboy, Anna.

In his voice came the answer.

A crazy cowboy, her thoughts added. A crazy cowboy who could get himself killed by turning the wrong corner and wandering into the city's meaner areas.

And she'd let him go. Why? Why, for even a moment, had she let herself believe in cowboys and countesses and a love that could conquer all else—even reality?

She was a bigger fool than Kent. He had the excuse of amnesia. She had no such alibi. She had only her heart.

A heart that had asked *What if? What if Kent was the one for her as her heart demanded and her head dreamed? What if they'd been given this one chance—one final chance at happiness? What if she blew it? What if?*

"Crap," she said aloud.

She switched on the radio to search for a traffic report and to quiet her thoughts. Still her questions mounted until they changed into reproaches, her apprehension mixing with anger at herself. If anything happened to Kent, it would be her fault. She'd let him ride off in the night. He'd sat on a hack of a horse primed for pasture, and she'd seen a steed. He'd worn jeans, tipped his hat, called her 'darlin', and she'd believed he was a cowboy.

She'd wanted to believe. There it was, pure and simple as Simon. She wanted to believe in cowboys and countesses, and a world where a corporate CEO and a cleaning woman were a perfect match.

She'd wanted to believe. And she had. Now Kent was hurt.

"Finally this morning, here's one fellow who's taken to heart those infamous words, 'My heroes have always been cowboys.'" The disc jockey's chatter broke through Anna's thoughts. "Police report a robbery in progress late last night was foiled when a man wearing a cowboy hat and riding a horse—that's right, folks, a horse—charged into the middle of the mugging and chased the alleged perpetrator. Police report the robber, later identified by his would-be victim, was found hog-tied to a telephone pole. Looks like L.A. has got its own Lone Ranger."

Anna swore again, swinging the van to the shoulder of the freeway, driving illegally past the inching traffic to her left. She took the next exit onto Sunset and followed the boulevard north.

Eventually she came to the hill-town homes, set back behind their long spine walls and high gates. She found Kent's residence as if she'd always known where it was. She pressed the intercom at the gate. Leon answered.

"It's me," she said, and the gates opened.

She followed the drive up. The road twisted, alternately revealing then obscuring the building at its end, as if the owner hadn't decided if visitors were welcome or not.

She stopped before a white rectangle, austere and unreal. A magazine-layout home. A place photographers shot pictures of, architect students studied and where men and women, slim and dazzling, stood in small circles in its rooms, wineglasses in hand, smiling closemouthed. A place where Anna didn't belong.

She parked the van and walked to the house. The views circled around her, freeing yet isolating. Leon answered the door.

"Where is he? Has an ambulance come? A doctor? Why are you still here?" She stepped in, then stopped, quieted by the sheer understatement of wealth, the careful presentation of style. She'd been to homes such as this before, but always as an employee. Never as a visitor. If not for an odd quirk of circumstance, she reminded herself, she wouldn't be here now, coming in through the front door.

She followed Leon into a wide, high-ceilinged room. She saw Lightning tethered to the steel rail of a back deck. "Why are you sitting down?" she said to Leon. "Kent needs medical attention. If an ambulance hasn't come yet, we'll take him to the medical center ourselves."

"He's sleeping," Leon told her from the vast folds of a long couch.

"Sleeping?" Anna's voice echoed in the large room. "He shouldn't be sleeping. What if he has a head injury?"

Leon, for once the calm one, eyed her. A small smile jerked his lips. "He already does, remember? That's what made us all one big happy family in the first place."

She paced the unbroken stretch of floor. "Which is why we've got to get him to—"

"Sit down." Leon beckoned from the wide swath of white sofa.

She stopped and looked at him as if she didn't understand him.

"Kent's not hurt. He's okay. He only has a few small cuts along his brow which, for all I know, were there from the first accident."

She collapsed into an interior decorator's dream of a chair. "Thank God."

"Thank God," Leon echoed.

"Wait a minute." Anger propelled her back up again. "What kind of a dirty trick was that? Do you know what you put me through?"

"Easy, Countess..."

"Don't you dare smile at me. Ronnie taught me a few roller derby moves that can make a grown man cry." She moved toward him.

"Wait a minute." He held up his hands. "I thought he was hurt when I first saw him, I swear. If you'd seen him before he cleaned up, you'd have jumped to the same conclusion. He'd had a bloody nose that was running like a river. There was blood all over him, but once he washed up, I saw he didn't have much more than a scratch. He was lucky...at least, this time.''

Anna sank into the couch's oversize cushions. "How'd he get the bloody nose?"

"'Wrestling a no-good rustler' was all he told me. I didn't know whether to believe him or not.''

"Believe him." She told him the radio report she'd heard on the way over.

Leon rubbed his face. "He's taking this code of the West thing too far.''

"Next he'll be trying to form a posse to round up the gangs in east L.A. You've got to make him stop," Anna insisted.

Leon looked at her through the length of his fingers. His smile was slow. "You care about him.''

"Don't be ridiculous," she returned too quickly.

Directly opposite, Leon eyed her.

"He's a human being," she put forth.

"Contrary to what some of our competitors and a few consumers say," Leon qualified.

"And yes, in that context—one human being to another—I don't want to see him hurt." She watched Leon's smile widen.

"He's in a vulnerable state right now. He's not safe, and he's riding around L.A. like he's Wyatt Earp.''

Leon looked at her. "Which is exactly why you've got to get him out of the city and up to the ranch.''

Before Anna could answer, Leon stood up, using the temporary advantage of height to lean over and look down at her. "If you weren't so in love with him, you'd do it in a second."

She stared up into his eyes, his lashes so pale as to be nonexistent. "Bull."

She stood up. Leon didn't move an inch, but any momentary advantage he'd maneuvered was gone.

"I'm not in love with him."

"Then go," he dared her.

"No."

"Give me one good reason." Leon's smug expression taunted her.

"The business."

"The business will be fine. In fact, several new clients will be calling today—some of the Hills' most influential ladies, several fair-sized companies. Did I mention that Landover Technology is looking for a new independent service?"

Anna forced her expression smooth. The Landover Tech contract alone would secure the Clean Queens' success. Her mother, who had struggled her whole life, would never have to worry about money again. Still, it was a bribe, and that wasn't the way Anna and her mother did business.

"Thank you, but the Clean Queens will succeed without your generous assistance."

"This isn't generosity. We compared, and your prices are lower than our current cleaners, but make no mistake, if the job isn't done well, it's goodbye Clean Queens."

"Don't worry. The job will be done well."

"Good. Then neither of us will have anything to worry about. I'll stay in L.A. and prepare for the Japanese contingent to arrive, and you, Countess, can go to the ranch and cowboy with Kent."

She hesitated, searching for an excuse.

"He was lucky last night. It was bad enough he was risking public exposure by staging a Gene Autry act right outside your bedroom window, but now we've got bigger worries than publicity. If the man he lassoed last night had been quicker or had a partner, Kent could've been seriously hurt...or, more likely, killed."

Anna remained quiet. She knew Leon was right.

"I'm sure it won't be more than a week or two before his memory returns," Leon noted. "Who knows? It may be sooner."

"It could be later." She finally spoke.

"Either way, the final line is, one day his memory will return."

What then? Anna had to wonder. What then when he looked at her and saw, not a svelte, elegant countess but a gangly, mop-topped maid? What then when her heart was destroyed, her dream gone for good?

Still, Leon was right. Considering Kent's current state of mind, he wasn't safe in L.A. If she didn't go with him to the ranch, and something happened to him here in the city, it would be her fault. She'd be to blame. She'd learned that lesson this morning. She had to think past her own concerns, set aside her selfishness. For Kent's sake. With the promise of coming contracts, the business would be busy, but she knew her mother and Ronnie could handle it without her. She had no excuses—except for her fear of her feelings for this man. Yet it was those exact emotions that told her she couldn't sacrifice this man to save herself.

"Maybe he'll wake up this very moment, memory fully intact, and everything will be back to the way it was," she put forth, still not ready to concede.

Leon nodded. "Yes, he could. But if he doesn't…?"

He watched her, waiting for her answer. She looked around the pristine room, its sterile colors, its cool beauty. "This place must be a bitch to keep clean," she commented, stalling for time.

"Anna," Leon said. Restrained impatience cracked his voice. "If Kent wakes up still believing he's a cowboy, and you his beloved countess, what are you going to do?"

She looked from Leon to the wall of windows. Outside, Lightning lifted his head and swung it slowly toward her. He looked right through her, as if he alone could see her core, the essence that had always belonged to Kent, and none other—not even herself.

What could she do? She looked into the horse's old eyes, watery and wise.

"I'll go," she said.

THE HIGHWAY STRETCHED straight to the horizon. Past the metal rails on both sides, the land lay low, silent, shouldered by distant mountains. The shad-

owed colors of buildings and streets had given way
to the green and gray of wooded valleys, and there
were long moments when Anna couldn't remember
why she'd fought so hard to stay in L.A. They'd left
the city's crowded, towered streets that morning, and
as the buildings shrank and the land loomed, a sense
of rest seeped in. Her bones seemed longer, leaner,
her body languid. Her speech took on a drawl. She
cushioned her head on the back of the truck seat and
looked to the full blue of the sky. A pair of hawks
circled on rising warm air. So still was her heart, so
quiet was her mind, she might have been a traveler
at the end of a long journey.

Less than two days ago she'd told Leon she'd go
with Kent to the ranch and had watched the relief
spread over his thick, square features. Then, miscast
within the vogue rooms, she'd waited until Kent
awakened. When he'd finally come into the win-
dowed room, she'd turned to him, half hoping, half
fearing he'd growl, "Who the hell are you?"—signaling he was cured, his personality and memory restored. But when she saw him look blankly around,
as disoriented as she, she'd placed her hand on his
forearm and said simply, "I'd like to go to the
ranch." He'd looked even more stunned for a moment. He'd said nothing. Then his expression had
gone to joy, and she'd known that whatever was to
follow would be worth the minutes of raw happiness
witnessed on that man's face.

Her mother, knowing Anna's mixed feelings on the
matter, had been cautious in her delight, but delighted

nonetheless. Ronnie had been uncharacteristically quiet, only telling Anna not to worry about anything and to call immediately if she needed anything. Early this morning she'd hugged them both hard, then waved goodbye, watching them from the cab of Kent's Chevy until they were out of sight.

The Rocking Horse Ranch was far north, near the Oregon border. Kent expected they'd be there by late tonight.

"It's pretty," he told her as if he'd lived there all his life. "There's a house, white clapboard. It probably needs a new coat of paint. I'll paint it whatever you wish—white, blue, purple, polka dots with striped shutters."

She smiled. "White is fine."

"Some flowers might need to be planted where the house's hard edges meet the ground, but it's got a wide porch stretching along the front where you can sit in the shade."

He paused. His eyes watching the road had taken on a softness. "It's got a pasture full of cattle. Beyond the corral, a bluff rises. From its top, you can see the river's curves and the mountain's snow and your entire world before you."

She listened to his words, her head and body growing heavy, fat with content. She knew if she closed her eyes, she, too, would dream of the Rocking Horse Ranch.

They drove on, leaving farther and farther behind the reality she'd known. When she looked behind her, she'd meet the silent, stoic stare of Lightning. When they stopped to get gas and a soda and fresh water for the horse, Anna saw her own eyes as full as a rustlers' moon in the rest room's distorted mirror.

Their bellies full from the soda bread and muffins Anna's mother had packed, they didn't stop to eat a meal until late afternoon. They exited the interstate and drove in a long loop to a low string of stores with strips of dirt for parking. Men in cowboy hats drove most of the pickups and trucks they passed. Some lifted their fingers from the wheel in a three-digit salute. A diner sat beside a gas station. Two men in high-crowned hats leaned near the diner's front door. Kent pulled in to the dirt lot and parked. Anna got out of the truck. She heard Lightning shift in the trailer's narrow stall. The two men watched the couple approach, returning Kent's nod as he and Anna passed. Anna knew as she and Kent walked on, the two men continued their scrutiny, leaning against the building, arms folded.

She and Kent sat down at a freckled counter and ordered cheeseburgers and sodas. That morning, Anna had woven her hair into a single braid down her back, but still strands had resisted. They curled about her face and the length of her braid, and feather-edged the Atlanta Braves baseball cap she wore. Kent was dressed like the other men in the diner: dusty boots, faded jeans, silver-buckled belt, denim shirt, cowboy hat, bandanna wrapped loose around his throat. He lacked only the perfect circle brand on his backside created by a can of chewing tobacco creasing his rear pocket.

"Just passing through, folks?" the waitress asked, setting two Cokes and straws down before them.

Kent nodded. "Headed up north, near the Oregon border."

Anna saw the waitress look at the large cowboy left of Kent two seats down. The cowboy swiveled his stool toward them, looking at them.

"Headed up to the ol' Lewis place?" he asked. A toothpick bobbed in the far corner of his mouth. Even sitting down, he was a monument of a man.

"Rocking Horse Ranch," Kent answered with a sidelong glance.

The cowboy nodded. "That's it." He studied Kent some more. "I've heard some talk about that spread."

Kent looked straight ahead, took a sip of Coke, said nothing.

"I heard the place was bought by some rich city dude." The man's voice was a deep boom, reverberating from the depths of his barrel chest.

Kent nodded. "I heard that, too, but it's a mistake."

The man chewed on the toothpick. "A mistake?"

Kent turned to the man. "A cowboy bought it."

The big man studied Kent. "That's not what I heard. I heard the owner can't tell the difference between a horse and a cow. You can buy the entire state of Texas, but you can't just strap on spurs and call yourself a cowboy."

Kent shrugged. "No one's born a cowboy. That don't mean you can't become one." He picked up the cheeseburger placed on the counter before him and took a bite.

The cowboy shook his head. "Tough place to try. The family fought over what belonged to who, and how to get the biggest share, even before they put ol' Jed Lewis in the ground twelve years ago. Meanwhile, the spread was left to take care of itself. Cowboy or tenderfoot, this new fella is going to have his work cut out for him. If he's going to get the Rockin' Horse up and running smooth again, he's going to need the best foreman west of the Mississippi."

Kent poured catsup on his fries. "And who would that be?"

The cowboy smiled slow. "Me. Mountain John." Across two stools he reached out an arm solid as an oak and extended a slab of a hand. "I'm heading up that way, too. I worked the Circle D up in those parts for many a year, but got to feeling too settled, and it scared me. Loaded the Dodge and my cow pony, kissed my favorite girl goodbye and headed north about four years ago. Last time I passed through here was about a year ago. Guess I got homesick, though, 'cause here I am again. Steady work is scarce in these parts, what with most of the ranches family-run or going broke. I figured the Circle D would take me back, but when I heard a city slicker bought the ol' Lewis place, I figured there's a challenge to make me feel young again. Whaddya say, partner, maybe together we'll be able to save this sorry dude."

Kent laughed out loud as he took the man's hand

and pumped it in a hearty shake. "I pray to God, Mountain John."

The slow smile stayed on the big man's face. His hand still clasped Kent's. "Did you hear about the boss's missus?"

"The boss's missus?"

Mountain John released Kent's hand to slap his rock-solid thigh. "This is the best part—even better than a tenderfoot taking over the Rockin' Horse. It seems the missus is some sort of royalty—a queen or princess or some such foolishness."

Kent glanced at Anna and winked. "I heard she was a countess."

"So, you did hear?" Mountain John released a rumbling laugh. "Countess, princess, duchess? Don't matter, you still can't beat it."

Kent looked at Anna again. "I don't know. Sounds to me like this fellow might be a very lucky man."

Mountain John's laughter rolled like slow thunder. "Lucky? A Monkey Ward cowboy in the corral and royalty in the ranch house? Why, I'd work for free just to see it."

Anna looked at the bear of a man, adopting his friendly smile. "Oh, don't worry, Mr. Mountain, we'll pay you, won't we?"

Mountain John looked at Anna, then back to Kent. "We?" He was still smiling.

So was Anna. She pointed at Kent. "The cowboy." She pointed at herself. "And the countess."

Mountain John's laughing features fell. He looked at the couple for a long moment, then leaned his huge body back, slapped his thigh once more and let forth his booming laugh. "And I'm the King of Siam."

Their meals finished, Kent picked up the check and stood.

"Wait a minute," Mountain John said. He rose, tall and thick as a redwood. "You two are serious? You're the new owners of the Rockin' Horse?"

Smiling amicably, Kent nodded and went to pay the bill. Mountain John stared down at Anna. She smiled up at him.

Kent came back, clapped the big man on the back. "It was a pleasure to meet you, Mountain John."

The man spread his broad hands in an apologetic gesture. "Folks, no insult intended. It's just, well, you've got to admit, the whole thing, it don't make any sense. It just isn't reasonable."

Kent smiled. "Reason isn't always right, Mountain John."

He took the man's hand once more. "I hope you'll join us."

Mountain John looked at them. The rest of the diner was silent. Kent and Anna walked out into the night that had come. Kent checked on Lightning, gassed up the truck and had looped back toward the interstate before Anna spoke.

"He thinks we're crazy." She gave a quick laugh. "Everybody in that diner thinks we're crazy." She looked out to the darkness blending the lines of heaven and earth. Her laugh was longer this time. "Hell, I think we're crazy."

Kent reached over, found her hand pressed against

the flat of the seat and took it in his own. "We might be," he said.

He looked at her. "Reason isn't always right."

The grip on her hand was sure and strong and warm.

"Believe in us, Anna."

She looked at the man in profile beside her, his features illuminated by the flash of passing headlights, then receding back into the night's soft drape.

He made such perfect sense, how could she not help but believe?

And wonder when and where she'd lost her mind.

Chapter Eight

It was past midnight but still hours from dawn when they arrived at the ranch. The unbroken highway and the night had lulled Anna into head-bobbing bouts of sleep. She'd awaken with a stabbing pain between her shoulders and the feeling she should be remembering the images in her dreams. Then she saw a sign up high, arching blacker and stronger than the night: The Rocking Horse Ranch—and she wasn't sure if she was awake or dreaming. All she knew was the fear within her grew small.

She smiled, and when Kent looked at her, he was smiling, too. They passed beneath the arch, and her vision blurred. Turning away from Kent, she blinked, releasing fat foolish tears.

They drove over a mile of dirt road before Anna saw much else than the night. Then the Chevy rounded a wide curve, and a sprawling two-story house appeared, its front porch facing the mountains.

Behind it was land divided by fences and several gray-weathered buildings in various sizes and stages of deterioration. She saw barns, sheds, grain bins. Far to the left sat a pair of narrow mobile homes. Beyond them was another long building, one corner of its low roof sagging. But it was a closet-size building set back not far from the house that held her attention.

"This place has running water, doesn't it?" she asked, still staring at what looked like an outhouse.

Kent chuckled. "You city gals…"

"Please let there be indoor plumbing," she pleaded.

Kent softly laughed again. "I know it looks rustic, but don't see just what's there—see what can be."

Her apprehension grew. "All I want to see is a toilet with a flusher."

"Don't worry. It has indoor plumbing." He shot her a smile.

He parked at the end of the curved dirt driveway beside the house, cut the engine and removed the keys. He slapped his palms against the steering wheel. "We're here," he said, as if he didn't believe it either.

He looked around a minute longer, taking in the house, the buildings, the space and the silence. His palms hit the steering wheel once more as if his emotion demanded physical expression.

Smiling, he looked at Anna, then opened the truck door and jumped down. She reached for her own door handle, but it was already swinging away from her. Kent stood on the other side, holding the door. He took her elbow as she slid out of the truck. "I'll unload Lightning, then get our stuff in a minute. You probably want to look inside first.'' He winked. ''Find that toilet.''

He handed her the keys, showing her which one was for the house. ''The real estate agent only sent me the back door key for now. They haven't found the front door key. Previous owners can't remember ever locking it. Seems they don't have much use for front doors out here. Everyone comes in through the kitchen. Let me get Lightning bedded, and I'll be in.''

Anna walked the short distance to the house while Kent unloaded Lightning and began to lead him to one of the grayed buildings. She unlocked the back door and felt around the door frame for a light switch. She found one and flipped it up. The backyard flooded with light. A dog began to bark. She looked behind her but saw only Kent and Lightning, buildings and land. Kent looked back at her, gave her a thumbs-up sign.

She flipped the switch next to the first one and an overhead light came on, revealing a small, square room with several benches, a deep sink and a row of hooks along its walls. Beyond it was the kitchen lit by two long tubes of fluorescent light that flickered on once she found the switch. It was a large room, narrowed only by a massive, rectangular table of rough-hewn wood surrounded by enough oak chairs to seat twelve. A chipped, white enamel gas stove took up one-third of a wall. At the opposite end an old-fashioned refrigerator, its finish yellowed, occupied a corner. There were no curtains on the windows. She swore she smelled beef gravy.

She pushed open a door and entered a room vast even in the constricting darkness. She walked to a small table and switched on a brass lamp, its finish gone green. The light spread out and was swallowed by the room's dark-stained wood walls and wide knotty floorboards. The high ceiling above stayed in darkness; the wide, railed landing that overlooked the whole room was silhouetted. A pair of Navajo rugs, swimming in the sea of dark wood floor, were spaced equally. The furniture was solid, scarred oak, coated with dust. A stone fireplace lined one wall. The rest were bare. In the far corner an open staircase led to the landing. She climbed the stairs and was standing on the platform above, looking down into the room, when Kent came in. He looked up.

"There you are. Isn't this something?"

She didn't know how to respond. "Something," she agreed.

He looked around the sober room, nodding and smiling. "Let's see what's upstairs," he said, and started toward the staircase.

Upstairs were three bedrooms and a bathroom. The bedroom in the northeast corner was the largest, made even more so by the simple, sparse furniture in it: a high, thin bed with a scrolled maple headboard and a faded quilt cover, a small stand and a tall pine dresser. In one corner was a solid-color armchair, its cushions sagging inward. Beneath the windows was a slender pine table and chair and a wrought-iron lamp. The darkness outside the window deepened and dipped down, then rose, shaping the soft diagonals of the valley beyond.

Kent nodded, touching everything as they passed as if he needed to feel them beneath his fingers. He hadn't stopped smiling.

The other two rooms were smaller, separated by the bathroom. The furniture was similar—sparse, plain, wood—except for a rusted iron bed frame in the bedroom at the end of the hall. Its quilt was thin, and the fabric's wine-colored roses had lost their bloom.

The house could not have been more different from Kent's sleek, self-conscious L.A. home.

She followed him back to the stairs, watching for his reaction. Before they left L.A., Leon had talked to several specialists, who had advised that the stark contrast between the ranch and Kent's previous life could be such a shock to his consciousness, his memory might return in sheer self-defense. Was this the moment, here in such foreign surroundings, when reality would restore Kent's memory? She heard him humming as he moved down the stairs, his hand skimming the length of pitted rail. She followed him, watching.

Reaching the living room, he went to its center and stood beneath a wagon-wheel light suspended above. He looked left, right, all around him and nodded. "We're here, Anna. We're home."

He looked at her. His arms reached out for her. She had taken a step when the kitchen door swung open, pushed by the long, skinny barrel of a shotgun. At the gun's other end stood a man no more than five-feet-eight-inches, bare chested, his skin dark and leathery, his body wrinkled and wiry. His face was grizzly with beard; his hair was the blackest Anna had ever seen. He wore jeans with frayed hems and un-snapped at the waist as if he'd pulled them on in a hurry. His one eye was closed, his other beady and black as it squinted at them through the gun's sight.

"Can I help you, folks?"

Kent started to step forward.

"Not so fast," the gunman said. Anna heard the click of the hammer. The sound echoed within her, the taste of fear in her mouth cold and dry. Kent stopped.

"You can as good as explain from there as here," the man said.

Kent smiled closemouthed as if he was the target of an expected welcome instead of a gun barrel. He lifted his hands chest high, his palms facing out, but his stance was wide legged and steady. "I'm the new owner of the Rocking Horse Ranch."

The old man's one-eyed gaze moved back and forth between Kent and Anna. "They told me the owner was some big-shot suit and tie."

"That mistake has been made before."

The man's squint narrowed. "You're standing there, telling me you're the new owner of the Rocking Horse Ranch?"

Kent nodded.

"From L.A.?"

Kent nodded.

"Prove it."

His palms still signaling no threat, Kent started once more toward the old man. "Out here, a man's word should be enough."

He continued forward until his chest met the press of the shotgun barrel. Anna watched, her own fear moving through her until she swore she could smell its shameful singe. The shotgun stayed square and steady on the other man's shoulder.

"Shoot me if you must, old man, but don't insult me."

Slit eyed, the man stared at Kent. Anna felt the wingbeat of fear within. Only silence sounded without. The man's wizened face, braced against the gun, drew tighter and tighter together until both eyes almost closed, and the man's features crumpled into a smile.

"You're crazy, you know that, boy?" the wrangler said.

The gun still tight to his heart, Kent nodded once. "That's been said before, too."

The man raised his head from the rifle. "I've been a cowboy all my life, and I've been around cowboys all my life, and no matter where they hail from or where they're headin', a cowboy has two things—a horse and guts. I seen your trailer outside...." The shotgun slid off his shoulder. "And I reckon I just seen your guts."

The man lowered the shotgun. "Your word's good with me, son." He switched the shotgun to his left hand and stuck the other one out. "Dutch McGee."

Kent took the man's knuckled hand in his own. "K. C. Landover. Glad to know you've been watching over the Rocking Horse."

"At my age, watchin' is about as close to cowboyin' as I git. When there's a full crew, I cook. When there's not, I cuss out those left."

"You've been with the Rocking Horse for a long time, Mr. McGee?" Anna asked.

The old cowboy turned to her. "Beg pardon, ma'am, but no one's called me mister for so long, I don't see any sense in someone starting now. Just 'Dutch' is fine by me."

"This is Countess Anna Delaney," Kent introduced.

"Just 'Anna' is fine by me," she also amended.

"So be it, then," Dutch acknowledged with a nod of his head. "Been with the Rocking Horse more or less forty years. Less when I was young and had the need to roam, more when these bones slowed and staying in one spot didn't seem the sin it once had. Been here steady the last twenty-one years."

"I saw the mobile homes. Your family here with you?" Kent asked.

Dutch shook his head. "Never married. When I was young, I was movin' too much for any woman to catch me. When I was old, I was too settled in my ways for any woman to want me.

"I had family in Jed Lewis, though. He was a good man. He had two sons, but both chose careers outside the ranch—one has an appliance repair shop up in Seattle, the other is an optometrist in Sacramento. Jed said they both done him proud and would never say otherwise, but ask me my opinion, and I'll tell you that the fact neither son chose the Rocking Horse when it came time broke ol' Jed's heart. After he passed on, his missus kept things going, but then the cancer got her. The two brothers asked the crew to stay on until the ranch sold, and most did as long as they could out of respect for Jed.

"Not many of us left now. Jed's boys took any profits and put them elsewhere instead of back into the ranch. As the situation got sorrier and sorrier, hands had to leave, look for better prospects. Can't say I blame 'em. If I was younger, I might've joined 'em. But I've been here so long, the Rocking Horse…well, it's like home."

The old cowhand paused, looked at Kent and Anna. "Seems the less I move, the more I seem to need to talk. What say I make you folks a pot of coffee rather than stand here flappin' my gums?"

"I could use the coffee," Kent agreed. "But I could also use the talking. All I know about this spread is what the real estate agent told me."

Dutch cracked a smile. "Took yourself a chance there, didn't ya, cowboy?"

Kent smiled back. "Once in a while a man's got to lead with his heart instead of his head."

"Sounds to me like a good way for a man to get himself into a big heap of trouble," the old man replied, leaning his gun against the wall. "Well, come on in the kitchen and I'll tell you what I know."

He pushed open the kitchen door, Kent and Anna following.

"Can I help?" Anna asked as Dutch went to the sink and began to fill a coffeepot.

"There's a can of coffee grounds in the door of the refrig."

She started toward the refrigerator.

"And you might as well bring out the condensed milk while you're there."

"How long you been doing the cooking?" Kent asked.

"Since Mrs. Lewis got sick. I used to do all the cookin' for the hands down in the bunkhouse, but when Mrs. Lewis died, after a while it seemed a shame, this big ol' kitchen up here empty and lonely, so I got permission from Jed's sons to do the cookin' here."

Anna set a small pitcher on the counter. She put the coffee can on the counter. "French roasted," she remarked, smiling at the first familiar thing she'd seen since she'd arrived.

"Just because we're rough around the edges doesn't mean we're completely uncivilized, Countess."

She looked up, hoping she hadn't offended the old man. Then she saw the teasing glint in his gaze.

"I don't suppose that means you have a cappuccino machine?" She exaggerated the hopefulness in her voice.

The amused light in the old man's eyes got brighter. "No, I don't reckon I do."

"That's okay." She shrugged. "Neither do I."

"Well, then…" He took the can from her and with his hand began to scoop the coffee into the pot's basket. "It looks like you and I oughta git along just fine, then."

He glanced over his shoulder at Kent. "There's a few other things we're without up here, also."

"I'd appreciate it if you filled me in," Kent said. "Like I told you, I don't know much except what I learned from the real estate agent."

"I'm sure it was a pretty picture painted for you, too, but like I said, ol' Jed been dead twelve years now, the missus eight, and not much has been put back into the place except enough to keep it going."

"How many hands are left?"

"Besides me, two. Gus Wannigan and Windy Jack. Gus is sweet on a schoolteacher in town or he would've been gone a long time ago. Of course, he'll call you a liar if you happen to bring that up to him. And Windy Jack—he rode the rodeo circuit when he was young, but a wreck with a blind bucker put a crick in his gitalong. He's a good worker—one bum leg ain't too bad when your horse has four, but he knows a washed-up rodeo rider isn't the cream of the crop when it comes to hired hands."

"The real estate agent said there were five men here."

Dutch nodded. "There was, until they got listenin' to all the talk in town. When the news spread the ranch was sold to some L.A. city slicker, everyone figured the Rocking Horse would either end up a dude ranch or a subdivision. The other two men decided they wouldn't stick around to find out.''

Dutch plugged in the coffeepot. "No offense," he said to Kent. "But you're not what we were expecting."

Kent smiled. "None taken. Confusion seems to be following me around lately like buckle bunnies at the national finals." He winked at Anna. She stared at him.

The coffee began to perk with a rhythmic beat.

"The herd's about a third of what it once was." Dutch opened a drawer and took out some spoons. "We used to run about eighteen hundred heifers, so the herd could be anywhere about thirty-eight hundred given the time of year. But the brothers didn't replace the sick ones, and when times got tight and cattle prices dropped, they'd sell off a few head to keep things going. Right now we're ranging about seven hundred."

He set unmatched mugs and spoons on the table beside the pitcher of milk. The smell of fresh coffee was strong in the air.

"We raised hogs for a time, but there's no place left to haul them to in California, so there was no profit. The land's too high for farming crops, but I keep a garden big enough to keep the crew's bellies full."

Dutch placed a sugar bowl and a tin of homemade oatmeal cookies on the table.

"So, we need men and cattle?" Kent asked, reaching for a cookie.

"And horses." Dutch unplugged the coffeepot and began to fill the mugs. "We've got seven, but four of them are smooth mouths."

"Smooth mouths?" Anna felt more and more as if she was in a foreign country.

"Old," Kent explained.

She looked at him again in amazement. *He's not a cowboy,* she told herself. *He's seen a lot of movies, read a lot of Larry McMurtry, and he learned to talk the talk. He's the owner of a computer company; I'm a cleaning woman.*

Kent stirred sugar into his coffee, completely at home. "What about the two trailers down by the barns?"

"Jed only needed one for the foreman he hired when he got sick, but he got a good price on the pair of them. Said the other one would be good if he hired a married man. Said they had a tendency to stay around longer. Truth be told, I think he was still hoping one of the boys would change his mind and come back to run the ranch. Anyway, the foreman stayed in one, and Jed told me to take the other, but I stayed in the bunkhouse with the other men until my bones said no more."

"Any of the men here now married?" Kent asked.

"No, all lone rangers, but since there's only three of us left, I let Gus and Windy Jack draw straws on the other trailer."

Kent took another cookie. "You know a man goes by the name Mountain John?"

Dutch nodded. "Worked the Circle D for a good

many years before the need to wander got him. About a year ago he found out he's got a little buckaroo back here. The mama don't want much to do with Mountain John anymore. Says all cowboys are good for is breakin' hearts. She's dating the postmaster. Mountain John thought it best he let them live their lives, but when I heard he'd headed out, I knew it wouldn't be for long. For him, the sun rises and sets on that little fella of his.''

''We met him earlier tonight. At a diner where we stopped for supper. He said he was heading up to the Rocking Horse for work.'' Kent glanced at Anna with a small smile. ''Seems he heard the rumors, and he's 'intrigued' by the situation up here.''

''Whether or not he shows up...'' Anna remembered the big man's confused expression as she and Kent had left. ''Remains to be seen.''

''You'd be a lucky man if Mountain does come. The man's heart is bigger than he is. And he can outwork the best of them. Outeat 'em, too,'' he added. ''He shows up, I'll be making a trip to town for supplies.'' He looked at Kent. ''Tomorrow, I imagine you'll be wanting Gus and Windy Jack to show you the operation.''

Kent nodded.

Dutch stood up. ''Seein' as how tomorrow's about come, I'll help you bring in your gear and then let you folks alone.''

Anna carried the coffee cups and spoons to the sink and wiped off the table and counter. After the men brought all the bags into the living room, Dutch retrieved his gun and said good-night. Kent walked out with him to check on Lightning.

When she finished cleaning up, she switched off the kitchen's harsh overhead lights, leaving the bulb over the oven burning for Kent. She went into the living room. The lone brass lamp she'd turned on earlier was still burning, forming shadows in the darkness.

A challenge to the illusion was the phrase Leon had used to describe how the unfamiliar atmosphere of the ranch would restore Kent's memory. She looked about her.

"It can't get any more challenging than this, Leon," she said, breaking the shadowed silence. "So tell me," she asked the night, "who's this great-looking guy in the cowboy hat and tight jeans talking about buckle bunnies and smooth mouths?"

She shook her head, running her index finger through the thick layer of dust along the sofa's frame. There was no answer, of course. She'd already known that.

At least, up here, he was safe.

She heard the kitchen door open and close. Kent came into the room.

"I needn't had checked on Lightning. He's doing fine. I think the ol' fella has his eye on a big bay mare already."

"What the heck are 'buckle bunnies'?" Anna blurted.

He looked at her a moment, then he smiled his slow-coming smile. He took off his hat and ran his hand through his hair. It had begun to grow. He'd worn it long when he was a child. In the summer, she remembered, it'd bleach white, his crown all curls and captured light, and he looked not a child but an angel. Then he'd turned six, and his father had had his hair cut so close you could see his scalp. She'd never seen his hair much longer since…until now.

"Buckle bunnies are the gals who follow the rodeo circuit."

"But how do you know what they are? And what 'smooth mouth' means? And how to tell a mare from a male horse? And what the heck is a Hereford/Cross heifer? And how did you drink that coffee? I'm surprised it didn't eat through the metal pot."

He didn't speak right away, as if waiting to see if she was through. Then he said, "Anna" in a tone gentle, loving.

And she was his.

He came toward her. She half turned her body away. But the rest of her, her reason, her heart, her desire, was his.

He placed a hand on her shoulder as if to calm her, and her heart quickened, her breath held. She tightened the skin along her mouth, attempted a similar defensive draw of her muscles.

"I know what's bothering you, and I don't blame you. I understand."

Her head swung toward him, and she stared at him over her shoulder. "You do?"

"You don't have to pretend anymore."

She looked at him. "I don't?"

"No. Neither do I."

It's happening, she thought. Just as the doctors and Leon predicted. His memory is coming back.

Kent smiled at her. "We should talk. Let's sit down."

He led her to the couch and brushed the heavy dust off the cushion. He nodded for her to sit. He sat down beside her. Their knees met at an angle.

"Maybe if we'd talked about it more before." He took both her hands and wrapped them in his. "Maybe it could've all been straightened out long before this. It should've never gone this far. It wasn't fair to you."

His memory was returning. Just as she'd always known it would some day. Just like she'd hoped for. Hadn't she?

He paused, looked down at her. He smiled, and she saw regret. "In our hearts we both knew this day would come, and when it did, we'd have to stop pretending."

Leon had said when the memory returned, it might be slow at first, but once recovery started, it could progress at a rapid rate.

Still smiling sadly, Kent leaned forward and kissed her on the forehead as if saying goodbye.

She closed her eyes. No, not yet, she prayed. No, not ever.

"I am who I am, Anna."

She opened her eyes. "Yes, I know." She reached up, curved her hand to his cheek. "I know who you are."

His mouth kissed her palm. "I wish it were otherwise. I'm sorry."

Her other hand went to him, touched the curls barely begun along his crown. "Don't apologize. There's no need. It wasn't your fault. It was beyond your control."

"If I could change things, I would, but a man can't be but who he is."

"I know," she agreed. She smiled, and her hands stroked his hair now, soothing him. "I learned a long time ago everyone has their place in this world. Some are up high, some are a little lower. No matter how we try to ignore it, the differences are there. It's the natural order of things."

"You knew all this, and yet you still came with me?"

"Leon and the others advised me once we got up here, the differences would be so strong, it might be impossible to ignore them. They were right."

"But you had doubts?"

"Oh, yeah. To tell you the truth, I thought the opposite would happen. That coming up here would only reinforce what we wanted to believe."

"You did?" He smiled again.

"Sure, why not? It could've gone the other way. And we'd be up here happily ever after."

"That's what you wanted to believe?"

She looked into the blue of his eyes. "At this moment, I don't know what I believe."

His lips came to her. The kiss was a lover's—slow and gentle and unreal.

"I'd be lying," she said, her lips moving against his, "if I didn't tell you a part of me wanted to believe it could go on like this forever. Even though I knew it was impossible. Even though I knew it wasn't fair to you or me. Still..." She tipped her head back, looked at the man she loved. "It seems neither of us is willing to let our illusions die gracefully."

He cradled her face between his hands. "It's better this way. Better not to pretend."

"I know."

His thumb stroked her cheek. "We're going to be okay, aren't we, Anna?"

She wasn't sure. She'd told herself all along it would end. Right from the beginning she'd known. She'd known, and yet, now that it had happened, it hurt more than she could ever have imagined. For one minute more, sixty short seconds, as crazy as it seemed, she'd give anything for the man in her arms to be a cowboy...and she a countess. If only to say goodbye.

She forced a small smile and nodded. "We'll be great."

He brought her face to his and kissed her. She kissed him back—one final farewell before he returned to L.A. and forgot her. One last goodbye to a world that never existed, never should have been except for the dreams of two children...now grown, now gone.

"I love you, Countess."

He said it sweetly—a fond, final goodbye to a special friendship, a special time. A bittersweet triumph. She couldn't deny him.

"I love you, too, cowboy."

"Then marry me."

Chapter Nine

He might have struck her, she pulled back so swiftly.
He looked at her face, her expression stunned, scared.
He called himself a fool.

It was not how he'd imagined they'd begin. He'd
looked forward to this day, imagining it even before
Anna had agreed to come. He remembered the real
estate agent showing him the listing, trying to recite
the details, but his hands had risen, asking for quiet.
Her voice had fallen away. He'd seen Anna and himself, here together, as they'd once dreamed. Here, surrounded by land and sky, there would be space
enough, time enough for slow, careful courtship.
They'd been apart for a long time. They needed to
come together slowly. Here they could create the
world they once knew. Here he would woo Anna.

This had been his dream during the too many days
in L.A. and the long drive toward their destination.

Finally they'd come home.

And now, before their bags had been unpacked,
before his love had even rested one night in her new
home, he'd acted a complete and utter fool. Without

thought, without reason, he'd blurted the most sacred of proposals and, by its abruptness alone, rendered it shallow.

He was as clumsy and coarse as they both feared.

She came near him, and he was struck senseless.

A complete and utter fool.

A man in love.

She looked at him now. He saw the delicate lines, the tender features, the airy spill of red-gold curls suggesting a fire might be set within that ivory tower. He saw the blackness of bewilderment in her eyes.

He'd dragged her here, away from her cosmopolitan home and family to a raw land. A beautiful land, yes, but to the new, it could prove hard and cold and relentless in its welcome. To a lady, used to a gentler way of life, it could be unforgiving.

Still, she'd come. Even though she, too, was keenly aware their backgrounds were opposed. He wasn't sorry that he'd finally spoken of their most formidable foe—the fact that he was a cowboy, coarse, unrefined, lacking in the world's genteel ways, and she was a countess, elegant, cultured, sophisticated. It had to be said, and he'd said it: *I am who I am.*

And even then, she'd answered with the belief that they could conquer these differences and live here happily. Even then, she'd spoken only words of hope, words of love.

And before her breath was finished, he'd demanded more.

He didn't deserve her. She knew it as much as he.

It was not how he'd imagined they'd begin.

He looked at her, apology in his throat. She stared at him, her eyes round and unbelieving.

He loved her too much.

"Please," he began, at a loss. "I'm a fool."

She shook her head, but her eyes stayed on him, incredulous.

"I didn't mean it…I mean…I did mean it. I know, I know, it's too much, too soon. But we've been apart for so long, forever. Then, to be this happy again when it was thought impossible. Now you're here, and I'm here and…"

He knew he was babbling and fell silent. He looked down where their knees still met.

She finally spoke. "You want to marry me?" Her voice trembled.

He looked up, met her eyes. His voice was steady. "Yes."

He saw confusion in her eyes. Her hand plucked at a loose thread on the cushion.

"Don't doubt, Anna. Believe."

She stared at him. She didn't speak. He was gathering his words once more when she said, "What do you remember? Tell me."

"I remember you." He raised his hand, about to touch her cheek, then thought, *restraint, time.* He dropped his hand.

"What else? Do you remember Hilary?"

He gave a short laugh. "Who could forget Hilary?"

He saw she wasn't laughing.

"You're concerned about Hilary? Believe me, there's no cause for concern there."

Still the troubled expression was in her eyes.

"Why Hilary ever thought we should marry is beyond me. She didn't love me. I didn't love her. I doubt if we even really knew one another."

"Do you remember L.A.?"

Now he understood. She'd seen the ranch, the isolation. Out here there were no megamalls, cineplexes, five-star restaurants. She was having doubts, but was reluctant to voice them.

He had to be honest with her. "I don't know if I could go back, Anna. I don't belong there."

"What about Leon? Landover Tech?"

He smiled. "Leon worries too much. Works too much. However, that's why Landover Tech is in the best hands possible."

"Do you remember your house in the hills?"

"Of course I remember it. I hate that place."

She finally smiled. It was a small smile, but it eased the tight stretch of her features and seemed to deepen her breaths.

Encouraged, he added his own tiny smile. "You hate it, too, don't you?"

He'd hoped to see her small smile widen. He was rewarded.

"I wouldn't want to clean it," she confessed.

Then, as quickly as it had come, her smile was gone. She looked down to her hands, folded ladylike in her lap.

He knew she was thinking of a time when the idea

of cleaning houses would have been foreign to her—as foreign as him in a big leather chair behind a desk directing one of the world's largest computer companies.

"It's been hard for you, hasn't it?"

He said the words softly, but still, her head snapped up.

"I wish I could promise you the hard part was over, but you and I both know I'd be lying. It won't all be smooth sailing. We come from different worlds—you and I."

He watched her expression. Had she wished he'd never brought it up? He knew she would never have been so insensitive as to introduce the subject of their differences. Still, unspoken or not, the fact remained. She'd been brought up in privileged households. She'd been schooled in fine manners, exposed to the best, bred with aristocratic tastes and destined to marry within her class. Her intended was to be a gentleman of similar background and, hopefully, in light of her family's unfortunate circumstances, superior wealth. Certainly she was never schooled and bred to marry a man who kicked manure chunks off his boots at the end of the day.

"Our worlds are day and night, no question." He saw her hands tighten on one another.

"Now I'm asking you to give up everything else you know and come into mine. I know what I'm asking. I know it can't be easy."

He looked into the soft colors of her eyes. When her beauty astonished him as always, and his head had trouble forming a coherent sentence, he willed the words from his heart.

"I only know one thing. I love you, Anna. I love you. And I'm ninety-nine-point-nine-percent certain you love me. When you finally said it, I got so crazy with joy and excitement, I wasn't thinking. I scared you, I know, asking you to marry me like that. Scared you so bad, you're probably 'bout ready to walk back to L.A., if you can't find a way that's quicker."

She didn't smile, but nor did she tighten her features until her forehead wrinkled. She sat still and listened.

"Now, don't worry. I don't expect an answer to that question. Not this time. And I'm not going to ask you again to marry me...not right away, anyway."

He tried out a smile on her. She sat expressionless and listened. "We've been apart a long time, and we have to take the time to catch up, see what the years apart have done, tell each other all that's happened, and all that we hope will happen. We've got to learn what makes us happy or sad or angry. And we will— right here. We've got the time and the privacy. I can promise you that."

Her soft eyes watched him, waited for him to continue.

"What I can't promise you is perfection."

She shook her head.

"Yes, I know you don't expect it, but you deserve it. What I can promise you is I love you, and I'll do everything possible to make you happy. And I know you love me, too.

"I believe in us, Anna. And now I know you believe in us. That's all we've ever needed—belief. The rest will come.

"So, don't worry. I don't expect an answer. And I won't ask you to marry me again—at least, not tonight."

She didn't trust her voice, nor did she know the words to respond. All she knew was ten minutes ago she'd thought she'd lost him forever. She'd thought his memory had come back, and K. C. Cowboy was no more than a strange medical phenomenon. So sure was she, she'd said goodbye even as she'd wished for him to stay.

Then he'd uttered, *Marry me,* and she'd had no idea who said the words: CEO or cowboy? Even now she had no idea who the man was before her.

All she knew was she loved him.

"Who are you?" she had to ask. "Do you know?"

He smiled as if he didn't find the question odd. "Without you, I'm nothing. With you, I'm all things possible."

"What do you remember?" was all she could ask again.

"I remember you."

"What else?"

"There is nothing else."

CEO or cowboy, he kept talking like that, looking at her like that, and she'd take his hand and not let go. She'd take his hand and lead him to the room upstairs with the rusted iron bed and mute-colored quilt. And she'd not let go.

Definitely time for a new tactic. She remembered how, as a cowboy, he'd been mystified by computers, where as CEO of Landover Tech, he was a computer expert.

"Can you tell me what a hard drive is?"

He smiled at her, but she saw he was puzzled. He ran his fingers through his hair. "I'd say trying to climb a muddy hill with three flat tires and a trailer-load of fresh fertilizer."

She chuckled. It was still her cowboy sitting beside her. Her cowboy come home.

Whether his memory had really started to return a few minutes ago or she was so afraid, she'd seen signs where there were none, she didn't know.

She also didn't know if, in her fear, she'd heard his proposal and wanted so badly to make it real, she'd believed his amnesia gone, believed he was Kent Landover and he loved her still, believed they could live and love together happily ever after.

There was a lot she didn't know, except that Kent had been right about one thing: she did believe. Deep, deep down, she believed in him, believed in them. Against her own better judgment, against the odds, despite the reality, she believed.

Sweet, flawed faith.

"It's been a long day," Kent said. "We need some rest."

Oh God, yes, she'd never been more tired.

He insisted on carrying her bags upstairs. He wanted her to take the bigger bedroom that looked out onto the valley, but she insisted on the small one with the iron bed.

He brought in her bags—a black vinyl duffel and a silver nylon tote. She hadn't brought a lot. She didn't expect to stay long.

"You'll be all right, then?" He looked around the room, doubtful.

"I'll be fine. You go. You need rest, too."

He grinned. "I won't sleep a wink."

Nor she, either.

"Go, now." Always telling him to go, always saying goodbye.

"Good night, Anna." He took her by the shoulders, kissed her forehead, the tip of her nose, her lips. Just as the kiss was about to deepen, he ended it. His hands still on her shoulders, he stepped back, putting an arm's length between them. His shirtsleeves were rolled up above the elbow. She saw the twitch of the veins in his forearm, the shudder of muscle.

"No, I shouldn't have asked you tonight to marry me. But that didn't mean I didn't mean it. And when it's right, I'll ask again."

She hadn't realized she was leaning toward him until he went to kiss her once more, and there was no distance between them.

"And you'll say yes."

Their lips touched. Her mouth parted as if answering yes now. Restraint, tenuous at best, folded. His arms wrapped around her. Their bodies met as if one. Their mouths opened. All that could not be said with words was told by touch. His tongue traced the edge of her teeth, the soft inside of her mouth, and she seemed to fall against him. He drew her own tongue into his mouth, sucked gently, and she was falling still, a heavy, warm weight low within her.

He ended the kiss. She was clinging to him.

He smiled down at her. "Tell me again why I promised I'd take my time?"

She couldn't remember either.

He brushed her cheek with his fingertips and sighed as he released her.

He turned back at the door. "Sleep well, Anna."

If only to dream of him.

WHEN SHE WOKE the next morning, her eyes opened and she knew exactly where she was, as if she'd slept in this narrow, high bed since she was a child, instead of for only a few brief hours.

The house was silent, but the light in the bedroom was full, indicating it was late. She rarely slept past 6:00 a.m., but the drive and last night's late hour must have drained her. She snuggled beneath the quilt. The bed, like the others, had looked hard and uncomfortable, but in reality was welcomingly firm. The cotton sheets lay smooth and starched along her body. She should get up. She closed her eyes, enjoying the drape of warmth on her body, the quiet. She thought of Kent, imagined him sleeping, not far. Or, perhaps, awake like her, thinking of her as she thought of him.

She listened. So quiet was the house, she swore she heard his breaths, even and long. Then she realized it was her own breaths echoing within her, making the quilt rise.

She got up, pulled on sweatpants to partner with the tank top she'd worn to bed. She'd left her silk robe home. She twisted her hair up, caught it in a wide clasp atop her crown and pulled the loose ends in a semicircle, so that the strands fell like a fountain.

Barefoot, she padded down the stairs to the big room. The floors were cool, but sunlight washed the walls. Curtains would have to be airy, sheer, balancing the weight of the dark wood and allowing in all the warmth of the sun. Perhaps no more than a brightly colored valance would be all that was needed.

She pushed open the door to the kitchen. In here, gingham, of course. Small yellow-and-white checks—a valance held by yellow satin ribbon ties above. Two café half curtains on the bottom...

Wait a minute, Martha Stewart. She slowed herself. A few days of Kent *cowboyin',* and his memory should come back faster than Mrs. Lindsay's greyhounds. There was no need for decorating plans.

Still, sunny yellow, pure white would be perfect, she thought, indulging herself. She laid her hand against the side of the coffeepot. It was unplugged, but the metal beneath her palm was warm. She went to the cupboard to get a mug. She'd paint the cupboards country blue and change the knobs to white ceramic with forget-me-nots.

The coffee poured out black and oily. Anna was deciding whether to drink it or patent it as an industrial-strength solvent when the back door opened and banged closed.

Dutch came into the kitchen, leaning backward from the weight of canned goods, stacked four high, between his wiry arms. He set the stacked cans on the center of the table.

"Mornin', Countess. I gather no pea beneath the mattress disturbed your sleep last night." He disappeared into the mudroom, only to reappear a few seconds later, this time loaded down with boxes of paper goods.

"And I see you're a firm believer in buying in bulk." She took a cellophane-wrapped, twenty-roll of toilet paper from the old man's arms.

Dutch set the rest of the items down on the table. Opening the door to a tall, narrow pantry closet, he peered inside. "Ain't no such thing as a quick trip to the store in these parts." He arranged some cans on one of the closet's lower shelves. "It's a butt-bumpin', two-hour ride on a two-lane road to the nearest big food store. So when you go, you make sure you git everything you need, and as much of it as possible."

He went out the door again. Anna followed, almost bumping into him on his return trip. The paper sacks he carried were stacked so high all Anna could see was the round crown of his hat. She stepped to the side, letting him pass. When he came back out and found her lifting supplies out of the back of his truck, he said, "Here now, princess, step aside and let me finish."

Her arms already laden, she trotted into the house.

He followed her with another armful of packages. He dumped the goods on the table and pushed his hat back off his brow. "You know, they say only a fool argues with a skunk, a mule or the cook."

She smiled at him. "So, who's arguing?" She headed back out to the truck.

"But," she said as he caught up with her at the truck's tailgate, "if I was, which one would I be arguing with—the skunk, the mule or the cook?"

"I reckon most people would tell ya all three." He cracked a wide smile and handed her a sack of potatoes.

A half hour later, all the supplies had been brought in and put away.

"There…" Dutch shoved the last can into the cupboard. "That oughta hold us all for a while—even with Mountain John on the feed wagon."

"How come you're so sure he's coming?"

He closed the door of the long, tall closet. "He's already here."

"He is?" Anna looked up from the paper bag she'd been folding.

"Saddled up and went out with the boys and the boss this morning to see the back sections. Was waiting for us when we woke, with his feet propped on the dash of his Dodge, his paint in tow. Says he needs work, and of course, there's the boy, but…" Dutch leaned forward as if sharing a secret. "I'd say you all have got his curiosity aroused." He leaned back, chuckling.

"If he's as good as you say, he's more than welcome." Anna finished folding the bag and laid it smooth on the table with the others. "We can sure use the help."

Dutch picked up the pile of bags. "I reckon I never did hear your story last night."

She smiled. "No, you were too busy trying to decide if you should shoot us or not."

His lips curled up, framed by his grizzled complexion. "Did I make the right choice?"

She looked at him levelly. "You've probably made worse decisions in your life."

He chuckled again. "That I have, Countess. That I have."

He tipped his head back, observing her from beneath the long slope of his hat. "It's not my nature to pry, lady—"

"It's Anna, plain ol' Anna."

"Plain ol' Anna, huh? I'm glad you don't stand on no ceremony, but you're going to be a big disappointment to the tongues waggin' around town if you don't put on an air or two."

She smiled. "Expecting something grand, are they?"

"We don't exactly ooze 'beautiful people' out here. Although a couple of counties over they do choose a Garlic Queen every summer."

"Well, I hope the locals won't be too disappointed, but I'm not a countess."

"You're not?"

"No." She wondered how best to explain without causing too much confusion.

"What are you, then? A queen? Duchess? Princess?"

"No, none of those things."

"Not according to the boss. Why, last thing he said this morning, before he left to ride with the others to the back ridge, was, 'I don't want anyone or anything disturbing the countess. Let her sleep.' And that's what I did. Even when that fella called, wanting to speak to you."

"Someone called?"

"Yup, heavy-breathing guy. Lee? Leo?"

"Leon?" Anna guessed.

"That's it—Leon. I told him the countess wasn't to be disturbed but would return his call at her convenience." Dutch smiled. "I sounded pretty good, huh?"

She smiled back. "Pretty good."

"I mean, you being the first royalty I've met and all."

"That's the thing—I'm not royalty."

"I understand." Dutch nodded.

She looked at him. "You do?"

"We don't recognize the royal system here in America. No bowing and shuffling here. We're a democracy. Created equal."

"That's true, but that's not it, either. 'Countess' is just a nickname," she tried once more to explain. "From my childhood. It doesn't have any meaning."

"It's your brand, Countess, and no matter how

badly you want to fit in around here, don't turn your back on who you are. People are loyal to their brand in these parts.''

''I'm not turning my back on who I am. I'm trying to explain to you who I am.''

''You don't need to explain to me. You came up here, didn't ya? Left behind everything and everyone you knew and came to a strange part of the country and a new way of life. That shows somewhere along those fancy bloodlines of yours, you've got good, strong pioneer stock.''

She started to explain again, then decided it would probably only cause more confusion. Instead, she conceded with ''I don't want or expect any special treatment.''

The old cowboy looked at her, sucking on a back space where a tooth should have been. ''I did teach all the cowboys to curtsy this morning.''

She laughed. ''You didn't?''

He smiled. ''Nah, but I might.'' His dark eyes danced. ''Royalty at the Rockin' Horse. 'Bout time we brought some class to these parts. But don't be fooled—it's not an easy life up here, even when a woman's used to it.'' He took off his hat and wiped his brow.

''Don't worry about me,'' she assured him. ''I'm as tough as you think.''

He looked up. ''I know you're tough, and I'm suspectin' you've got what every good ranch woman west of the Mississippi has—heart. The same heart that led you here, head over spurs in love with a cowboy. That's the heart that will make you last in this land.''

''In love? I'm not in love with Kent.''

''Then why'd you marry him?''

''We're not married.''

He stared at her a moment. ''You two are living together?''

''Yes. I mean, no.''

The old hand shoved his hat down on his head. ''I believe it's either one or the other.''

''A few days ago Kent had an automobile accident,'' she began to explain. She stopped, uncertain how much should be revealed of Kent's current mental state.

The cook gave her a long look from beneath his hat's brim, waiting.

''He was in the hospital.''

''In L.A.?''

She nodded. ''He wasn't seriously physically injured, but he did suffer a concussion, and his memory was affected by the impact.''

''He seems fine.''

''He is, overall,'' she assured the old wrangler. ''He just has trouble remembering some things. The doctors say it's temporary.''

The old cowboy looked at her. ''The boss has amnesia?''

''Selective amnesia,'' she explained. ''He remembers some things. Other things are a blank.''

''He seems to know you.''

She nodded. ''I'm one of the things he remembers.

In fact, he wouldn't leave L.A. unless I came with him, so that's why I'm here—to stay with him until he gets his memory back. I'm more like a security blanket than a soul mate.''

"What else does he remember?"

"He remembers always wanting a ranch, so he went out and bought the Rocking Horse. And he remembers being a cowboy."

Dutch looked at her. "A woman, a ranch, cowboyin'. Sounds like he's remembering the things most important to him."

"No. At one time, maybe, me, the ranch, being a cowboy, these things were important to him, but that was a long, long time ago. Lately, the things that were most important to him were business, making money, power. Then came the accident, and he's different now."

Dutch shrugged as he moved off toward the mudroom. "Maybe his head just had to stop remembering, so his heart could start."

Chapter Ten

Anna smoothed her hands along the back of her hips and arched her spine, releasing the tension. She'd sat too long at the sewing machine. She got up and went into the kitchen to get one of Dutch's homemade cookies. His snickerdoodles rivaled her mother's. In a week, she'd become addicted.

Out the window over the kitchen sink, she saw Kent in the corral astride the big bay. Several horses had been brought in during the past few days. Several men had also been hired, two of whom had headed out with Windy Jack yesterday morning on a calf-buying expedition to replenish the herd.

Kent swung his horse in a tight circle, stopping several feet from the plastic steer head mounted on a bale of hay. He reached for the coil of rope suspended from the saddle horn and snaked out a loop. Spurring the horse to a smooth lope, he lifted the rope and twirled it in a slow circle over his head. Focusing on his target, he let the lasso go. Anna watched it sail through the air, clear the steer's fake horns and land on its head. Kent gave a sharp tug, pulled the circle tight and smiled triumphantly at the head on the bale of hay.

Mountain John leaned against the open barn doors, a wad of tobacco bulging his lower lip. He spit and nodded his approval to Kent. Kent swung down from the saddle to retrieve his rope, his smile wider. Mountain John spit once more, then lumbered over to where Kent was curling the rope back into a loose coil. Taking the rope from him, he demonstrated a grip. Kent watched and nodded. Taking the rope back, he shook out the lasso. Mountain John reached over, adjusting Kent's fingers into proper position, then twisted Kent's wrist, palm in, palm out. All the while, Kent nodded and watched.

The men all called him K.C.; they called her "Countess." In a week, Kent had earned the other men's respect through his sheer determination alone. Dutch had told them about the accident and the head injury, so any lack in Kent's ranch skills was attributed to his amnesia. His knowledge of and genuine love for the cowboy way of life dispelled any lingering doubts. He had a ranch, horses, cattle, hands. He had become the complete cowboy.

A woman and a young boy approached the corral fence. Mountain John looked up at their greeting, then moved toward them, a smile lighting his large, dark features. The child was Mountain John's son; the woman was Sally, the child's mother. According to Dutch's reports, Sally had been persuaded that her son needed his father as much as the father needed the son. Dutch predicted it also wouldn't be long before the postmaster was a thing of the past. From the way the man and woman were looking at each other, Anna had to agree.

She saw Kent smiling at the couple as Sally lifted the boy over the top rail and into Mountain John's arms. After a quick hug, the boy unwrapped two soft, fat arms from Mountain John's neck and squirmed out of his grip. Wearing pint-size chaps and boots that came up past his knees, he toddled over to where Kent stood smiling, twirling the rope. From the first day they met, the boy had taken an instant liking to Kent. The feeling was mutual. As the child came close, Kent scooped him up in his arms. The boy's parents continued to look at each other over the fence.

The phone rang, startling Anna out of the idyllic scene before her. She picked it up, stretching the cord so she could look out the window. Kent was holding the boy up high, jostling him above his head. The boy was beautiful in his laughter.

"Rocking Horse Ranch," she said.

"Anna, Leon. What's happening up there?"

"Kent just lassoed his first steer."

Leon moaned. "In other words, no progress."

"Oh, there's progress. Kent's becoming one hell of a cowboy."

Leon swore. "The Japanese businessmen arrived yesterday. So far, I've been putting them off, but they're beginning to wonder where the head of the company is."

"You can tell them on a cattle drive."

"Very funny. A corporation stands to lose the deal of the century, and you're cracking jokes."

She looked out the window. Eyes shyly averted, Sally was laughing at something Mountain John said to her. In the center of the fenced circle, the child straddled the bale of hay. Kent sat behind him, waving his hat above his head, urging their pretend bull faster and faster.

"You should see him, Leon. He's really happy up here."

"I don't care if he's happy. I don't care if he's downright ecstatic. What I care about is closing this deal, and for that, I don't need a content cowboy. I need Kent Landover back the way he was before."

"Miserable, alone, unhappy?"

"How about nondelusional?" Leon countered. "Listen to me, I need Kent back with his memory intact. The Japanese men are only going to be put off so long with tours of Disneyland and the Hollywood Walk of Fame."

"Don't forget Rodeo Drive."

"Look, I realize Kent getting his memory back won't benefit you, but—"

"What's that supposed to mean?"

"It means I'm beginning to question your motives."

"Excuse me? Weren't you the one who begged me to come up here? Remember—*challenge the illusion…indulge the remote memory?*"

"Hey, it seemed the right course of action at the time. I had to get Kent out of L.A. to some place safe and away from inquiring minds. Don't make me worry I was wrong."

"Do you want me to leave? Is that what you're saying?" She looked out the window to where Kent and the child still rode the bale of hay. Leaving wouldn't be that simple.

"No, that's no good, either. He'd probably form a posse and track you all the way to L.A. Then we're right back where we started."

She softened as she heard the frustration in Leon's voice. She'd felt it many times herself.

"Listen, I need Kent," he appealed.

"Well, if it's any consolation, I think he is better."

"Does he have his memory back?"

"No."

"Then he's not better. I swear, between Kent and you and the Japanese and Hilary—"

"Hilary? What's wrong with Hilary?"

"She's driving me crazy. The wedding date is getting nearer, the RSVPs are rolling in and she's starting to panic."

Anna looked out the window. Kent had lifted the child to his shoulders, his hat on the young boy's head. His arm steadied the boy, one hand wrapped around his ankle, and the two cowboys, old and young, gazed up to where the sun met the land and the birds circled on nothingness.

"I want him well," she said. "But I want him to be happy, too."

"Being delusional isn't the same as being happy," Leon pointed out.

"So, being rational and sensible is?"

"Sanity does seem to be a primary factor."

"He's not crazy, Leon."

"No, but he's also not himself."

She was silent. She knew what Leon was saying was right. Then why did it seem wrong? She took a deep breath, looking out to the land, the horses, the men. When had she become so deeply drawn into Kent's world? When had the dividing line between reality and fantasy dissolved, so that all she knew was happiness?

"You're right," she conceded.

"Of course I'm right."

"Maybe I should leave." Even as she said the words, her heart clenched.

"No, not yet. Like I said, that's not the answer. Damn, I'd be up there myself if I didn't have the Japanese to baby-sit."

"Do you really think they'll make the deal without seeing Kent?"

There was a pause, then Leon said, "No. But I'm hoping Kent's memory will come back soon, and all my problems will be solved."

Kent was loping around the field now, the child still on his shoulders. The boy's arms circled Kent's neck; his head was thrown back with delight.

"I don't know, Leon. I don't know what's going to happen."

"You're making me nervous again. Do you know I have an ulcer the size of the Grand Canyon?"

Leon's exasperated sigh sounded across the many miles.

"Sit tight for now," he decided. "I'll check in again tomorrow. But if anything develops before then, call me. Understand?"

After she hung up the phone, Anna walked through the mudroom and stepped outside. She leaned against the house, the wood warm on her back. Near her feet were the thin beginnings of peonies she'd planted yesterday. Kent saw her and smiled. He began to walk toward her, the boy still on his shoulders. A face new, smooth; another below, older, lined; above and below, eyes of innocence.

Kent raised his hand and waved. The child did the same. She waved back to both the man and the boy as one hugged the other. Laughing, Kent lifted the boy off his shoulders and handed him to his father. He bent down to let the child put his hat back on his head. He was still smiling as he came toward Anna.

"The little buckaroo's here," he said. He stood beside her, looking back at the corral. The child waved, and he waved back. "He sure makes Mountain John a happy man."

"He seems to have taken quite a liking to you, too."

Kent took off his hat, rubbed his brow where the sweat formed. "We cowpokes, we understand one another, that's all."

He put his hat back on, looked out toward the land. She looked to his profile. His eyes were clear and blue.

"Let's take a ride. Lightning is getting fat and lazy."

"I was hoping to finish the living room curtains tonight," she said, wanting to be with him but afraid.

"The curtains can wait, but this day's almost gone."

Still she hesitated.

"If you're going to be a cowgirl, you've got to climb down off the top rail and get into the corral." He took her hand. "C'mon, there's not much time left."

She let him lead her to the stable. Who knew how much time was left?

They reached the tack room, the smell of alfalfa and horse seeming to widen Anna's nostrils.

"Okay, darlin'." Kent picked up a blanket laid upside down, revealing a saddle beneath. "Here's your throne."

He handed her the blanket and, lifting the saddle off the rack, started toward where Lightning stood watching them, ears lax.

"Hello, ol' fella," Kent said softly, nodding for Anna to spread the blanket smooth across the horse's swayed back.

Standing on the left side of the horse, all the time talking softly, Kent lifted the right stirrup leather over the seat and laid the saddle on the horse's back. Anna offered her palm, felt the velvet of the horse's muzzle as Kent tightened the girth under the animal's belly and lashed the saddle into place with a leather strap.

Once the horse was saddled and bridled, Kent

handed the reins to Anna, and she and Lightning followed him to the corral where the bay was already waiting.

Standing to the left side of the horse as he'd shown her, she slipped her foot into the stirrup and grabbed the saddle horn. She swung her other leg up across the horse's back and mounted. Kent had her stand in the stirrups so he could adjust the length, and when satisfied, he handed her the reins.

Their fingertips touched, and he stood a moment, looking up at her. She smiled down at him. He continued to smile up at her.

"What?" she finally wondered.

He nodded, pleased. "Now you're up high, closer to the clouds where all angels belong."

She gave herself the gift of several seconds before she looked away from him. When her gaze rose, she saw that the blue of his eyes matched the sky all around them.

"We should go," she said. "It's getting late."

THEY RODE SIDE BY SIDE until they reached the creek and the path narrowed. Kent took the lead, and they continued, following the curves of the water. Anna watched him in front of her, the easy way his body moved with the rhythm of the horse. She wondered when his memory returned and his days were spent sitting in a padded leather chair, would he remember the feeling of sitting in a saddle as if he'd been born there? Would he remember a horse beneath him like the rolling warmth of life? Would he remember her?

Where the creek ran shallow they paused to let the horses drink, then crossed and moved on into the lower valley. The grazing cattle looked up without interest as the horses and their riders passed. The spring had been cool, breezy, and the green of the meadow had only begun. The wildflowers and the weeds were shoots not fully sprung, and the rains had tilled the land, leaving the soil darker, stronger with smell.

The trail widened. He waited for her to come alongside him, and they rode aligned up a long slope past pine and cedar and fir. They stopped where the land leveled, and looked out to the creek curving below and the steep mountain front beyond. The mountains were already thick with shadows, the distant trees gone still and gunmetal.

They dismounted and, leading the horses, walked awhile. At a wide rock they released the reins and sat, backs propped against the stone, shoulders touching. They looked out over the valley while the horses nosed the ground nearby. The sun had lowered, tinting the sky a rainbow of red. Kent had been right. The day was almost done. She felt the long press of their thighs, the long want within her. She stared into the spreading blood-red sky.

"Keep it up, and Mountain John will have you riding point when we move the herd up to the mountains this summer."

She looked at him, knowing she would be gone long before then. More likely than not, he would, too. He misread her pained expression as confusion. "The point rider rides at the head of the herd like a pilot,'' he explained. "He's usually the top hand.''

She looked out to the stained sky. "Summer is a long way off.''

"Not so long. A few weeks.''

"Everything could change before then. Everything could change in a moment.'' They hadn't ridden high enough, and L.A. and Leon's voice had followed her.

Now it was Kent's turn to look at her, puzzled.

"Leon called earlier,'' she told him.

"Oh,'' was all he said. The confusion cleared from his features. His expression became unreadable.

They were silent for a few beats, then Kent said, "How is he?''

"You know Leon.''

Kent pulled at the brim of his hat. "He should come out here, get away from the city.''

"I don't think that's the answer.''

"No? Why not? I know you yourself had reservations, right?''

She nodded.

"And look how happy we are.'' He spread his arms, embracing the air. He looked at her. His arms fell. "You are happy, aren't you?''

The foolish part was she was happy—rare moments when she forgot and believed all this real, when she believed in Kent and herself and nothing else. She'd never been happier—except for one other time in her life. And Kent had been there then, too.

"As beautiful as all this is,'' she began, "the last

thing Leon wants right now is an invitation to the Rocking Horse Ranch.''

Kent leaned back and stretched out his legs, crossing them at the ankles, setting one scuffed boot atop the other.

''It may be the last thing he wants, but it's probably the first thing he needs.''

She smiled. ''I'm afraid even strapping on some chaps and chowing down on Dutch's chicken-fried steak wouldn't help Leon. He's pretty tense.''

Kent leaned forward, his hand touching the earth below them, sifting it through his fingers. ''It's understandable. What with the Sushima people coming into town for the big deal.''

Her head turned. She looked at him. The brim of his hat hid the top half of his face, but she saw his lips part, then tighten. His hand drew back from the land.

''You remember the Sushima deal?'' She meant her voice to sound hopeful, but it sounded hollow.

He pulled himself up onto the rock and sat hunched forward, his elbows resting on his thighs, his hands dangling between his knees. ''I guess I do.'' If he felt the same amazement as she, he was doing a better job of concealing it.

She looked out, seeing the sky had dried to reddish-brown.

''We should get back home,'' he said. ''The night's moving in fast, and soon we won't be able to find our way.''

Yes, home. She wanted to go home, far from L.A.

and Landover Tech and fast-talking partners and elegant, dark-haired fiancés who hovered like night dreams. She wanted to go home, run her hand along those scratched wood walls and rest on the iron bed newly painted white. The desire rose even as the semblance of shelter and safety began to shatter. Hurry.

"Do you remember anything else?" The question came out. She'd never felt so brave...or so frightened.

He stood, ready to go. "No," he said. A single syllable of complete unconcern.

But when she stood and looked up, she saw in his eyes, for the first time, the fear.

IT WAS THE SAME FEAR she saw later when he came and stood where the moonlight crossed her bedroom. It was inside them both now, moving like a disease. Even if he didn't remember anything else for many days from now, they both knew it was the beginning...the beginning of the end. She saw his fear and felt it inside her and she held out her hand.

They met in a fierce tangle of limbs and lips and sweet skin, smooth muscle, as if sheer physical strength alone could combat the fear begun. She was already naked beneath the faded quilt as if she'd known and was waiting. She couldn't be certain she hadn't known; she couldn't be certain her desire and fear, so deep, so strong, hadn't begun to silently sing, calling to her love.

He stripped off what few clothes he wore—a pair of jeans, briefs—and as he came back to her, she rose on her knees, stopping him with a smooth press of her hands on either side of his hips. There, in the moonlight, she worshiped him, her hands touching him reverently for the illusion he was. From his hips, her fingers followed the tight stretch of skin that was his stomach. She leaned down and kissed its center, felt it hollow on an inhale.

One more taste while her fingers moved on, climbing the rib cage, branching across the corded braille of his chest. Her lips followed. His moans met her own.

Now her fingers found his shoulders, curling into the dip of his collarbone, meeting in a circle around his neck, tracing a trail for her mouth to feed on as she lifted herself on spread thighs and pressed herself to him.

Her fingers went on, her lips followed, all with delighted defiance, feeling the illusion solid and hot and real beneath her touch. She spread shaking fingers into his hair, and her lips stopped, trembled open before his. *Soon* the parted flesh silently promised before moving on, needing to touch and taste more of him. Her mouth soft, she followed the curve of his face up one side and down the other, back to his neck, resting, gasping against the salty skin of his throat.

He said her name, a ripple of muscle against her open mouth, as he lifted her in his arms and took her mouth with his, meeting her passion so deeply she arched toward him, clinging as if she was falling, they were falling. They were flying.

He lowered her to the bed with its bright new coat of paint, his tongue full inside her, her own taste honeyed mead, his rich, thick malt. Their bodies blended, so solid, so real, the thick rush of blood throughout them, the damp sheen of sweat beginning.

But when he straightened his arms, raising himself to look down at her, the moonlight gilded him intangible, diffusing the skin into shimmers and shades of light even as his weight still pressed heavy on her, even as she slid her hand down the flickering, dancing surface of his flesh to find him hot, hard and pulsing with life.

His eyes closed above her. His head reared up, and even solid and firm above her, more real than anything she'd ever know, he was still all illusion, a fantasy. Her legs went wide with desire and demand came, the passion and the urgency. And the fear, always the fear that the dream would dissolve.

He opened his eyes, looked down at her, and she knew, at that moment, her breaths shallow, her lips pulled back with pleasure, she was beautiful. But he must have also seen the desperation, maybe felt it himself, for he reached to her brow, smoothing back the tendrils there, soothing with touch and a soft shush of breath until the frantic beat of her blood slowed and the mad dance of her heart steadied.

"It's all right, darlin'," he whispered, lowering his head, his kisses light as breath across her comforted brow. He rolled to the side, replacing his weight with the feel of the soft, slow heat of his mouth moving across her skin, her lips, suckling the rose-colored peak of her breast as his hand stroked between her parted thighs, began a bare, slow brush against the

tight, sensitive nub of her, each touch lifting her hips
in a pleading quiver. Sensation began in the hot hidden intimate folds of her flesh, and echoed where his
mouth tasted and teased her taut nipple, his tongue
licking in rhythm with his fingertip, bathing her in a
rising wave of pleasure, suspending her where all
things became both real and unreal until the delicate
coax of his tongue, his touch, took her tighter and
tighter, carried her higher and higher, and with a final
cry, sensation burst and she surrendered with a
spreading spasm of muscle, her fear ruptured, her
pleasure full.

Still liquid with sensation, still smiling, she drew
his weight back onto her and pulled him tight to her,
rejoicing in the hot, heavy feel of him, the press of
breath between their chests, the humming of blood in
their ears. Her legs were lax, embracing him, and she
guided him to the moist wash of her, tip meeting tip,
and her body arching once more, then releasing in a
shudder. She wrapped her fingers along the smooth
length of him, her legs spreading, opening wider, slip-
ping him into her, her hips rising once more.

His arms braced on either side of her, he looked
down, meeting her gaze, watching her. His thrusts
began so tortuously slow, she closed her eyes in a
dark meld of pleasure and need. She reached up to
him, bringing his mouth to hers, open, begging un-
ashamedly while her hips bucked, and the smooth velvet push of him quickened. Matching each other's
rhythm until the movements became driven and wild,
they called out a cry of surrender, shattering the

bounds of skin and separateness, soaring to the realm where reality and illusion meet and matter no more.

There they stayed, wrapped together, arms and legs twined tight, their skin silver in the moon's light. They didn't speak, knowing words weren't the answers here, nor had they been before. They lay still, breaths quiet, hearts calm, in the pale, mirrored light, holding on to each other gently as if fragile and newborn. Here, they lay undefined, vast, limitless. In each other's arms, they found freedom from what others saw, and what they saw. They shunned the covering of clothes, the inadequacies of words, the constraints of perception. Cradled together, they existed only for each other, and so aware, fell into sleep, their breaths feeding one another.

Chapter Eleven

They woke before the dawn, but the moonlight had already lessened from silver to gray, signaling the coming day. They embraced still; their faces turned to one another in the thick gray light and knew words had become necessary once again.

But first, a kiss, mouths sweetly mating, still tasting of the night before. And a gentle exploration of hands as if surprised that flesh once no more than shimmering sensation had become solid again. They touched, searching the boundaries of their bodies, their fingers lingering.

The grayness lightened. The day was almost here. Their time was running out. They knew they had to talk, to speak, make sense, make plans. Still they were silent, knowing now words were weak.

Anna smiled at Kent, and saw it returned. She stretched, feeling the fluid freedom of nakedness, dreading the confinement of clothes. Another barrier, she thought, reaching up, tracing the curve of Kent's temple.

He dropped his head to hers, kissing her long and

hard until the soft touch of their fingers turned sure and strong, and, rolling his weight onto her, he took her once more with the sleep still in their eyes and the night waning.

"I love you, Anna." He whispered the only words they needed.

"I love you, too," she whispered back, brave now with his body inside her.

Still, the night shifted into day. She lay on his chest, gathered in his arms, her fever cooled. She moved her cheek into the curve of his neck, blotting out the light, her lips lax against the touch of warm flesh, the moment perfect.

"We'll have to get up soon," she said, the words muffled into his neck. The day at the ranch began at dawn.

He stroked her hair. "There's time." He dipped his head, found her mouth. "Maybe I'll work in bed today."

She smiled. "That would take some maneuvering."

"Why not? I'll take this side. You can have this half." His arms wrapped around her, he rolled her to the left side of the bed. "See. I've got plenty of room for a laptop, fax...."

She felt every muscle go stiff. His arms around her, he felt it, too.

"Anna, what's wrong?"

"What did you just say?"

"I'm kidding. How much work do you think I'd

get done with you here in this bed?'' He draped a leg across her, tried to pull her close.

Her body resisted. "No, you said you've got plenty of room for a laptop...."

"Plenty of room to put you on top of my lap." His arms still tight around her, he rolled onto his back, bringing her on top of him.

She looked down at him. The stiffness stayed in her body. She could feel it in her features. "Fax?" she said.

"Facts?" he answered. His smiling expression became puzzled.

She rolled off him and sat up on the edge of the bed. She reached down, retrieved the quilt thrown onto the floor during the night. She wrapped it around her body, her back turned to the bed. She felt the touch of his hand on her back, and her spine arched.

"Anna?"

She looked at him over her shoulder. She made herself smile. "Your memory is coming back."

She looked into his eyes. He knew it, too.

Still, he shook his head. "I remember only you, Anna."

She turned toward him, placed her palm to the curve of his cheek. She loved him. "Soon you'll remember more."

He covered her hand with his. "What more is there? What more than this?"

She looked down at him. The cover fell from her shoulders, and silently she went to him once more. Words could not help them now.

"Evenin', Countess."

Anna stopped rocking and looked up from the potato she was peeling. Gus stood at the bottom of the porch, one hand on the rail, one foot on the bottom step. She couldn't decide if he was the tallest man she'd ever met or the thinnest. He'd been "split high" she'd heard the other hands tease him.

She looked past his lean shadow. The sun was still strong in the sky. "Not quite evening yet, Gus."

"Soon enough," he said.

Yes, soon enough, she thought, and began to rock once more.

He folded his narrow frame onto the top step. His shoulders naturally hunched, the long, bony curve of his spine pressing against faded denim. The ranch dog that had followed him waited while the man settled, then stretched out on the step below, his head finding the cowhide pillow of a boot.

Anna finished peeling the potato, cut it into chunks and put it in the pot. She reached for another from the seemingly bottomless bag beside the rocker. "Home early today," she said. The hands' days began at dawn and went eight, twelve, sixteen hours until the work was finished. No one on the ranch wore a watch.

"Day's not over yet. The boss and Windy Jack are still riding fence up along the northern section. Sent me and Mountain John down to meet a man coming by, looking for work. Mountain John recognized him from an outfit he worked a few years back, took him up to meet the boss."

"I thought enough men had been hired?"

"Never enough men, always too much work. Plus the boss is plum softhearted. Hates to turn anyone away. Good thing he's a cowboy. He'd probably go bust as a businessman."

Anna kept her gaze steady on the potato she peeled. "He knows how hard work is to come by these days, what with more and more ranches having to be completely family-run to make ends meet."

Gus propped his free foot up on one knee. "You're not a real rancher unless you're in debt up to your John B. But until they invent something that'll take as much abuse as a cowboy, I don't worry much."

Anna chuckled, rocked a little. Gus looked out across the spreading land. His hand spun around and around the rowel of his spur.

"Countess," he said. "I was wondering if I might ask you a question, you being royalty and all?"

"Now, you know once Dutch started calling me 'Countess,' it kind of stuck, and there was no way out of it, but I explained to you and the others, I'm no different than any of you. The 'royal' thing is a bunch of nonsense. Believe me."

"Still, ma'am, you're a real lady and all."

Anna looked down at the potato she was peeling. A pleased smile stole onto her face. "What'd you want to ask me, Gus?"

"Well, seems there comes a time when a man doesn't have much tumbleweed left in him...."

He paused. Anna waited.

He began again. "I was wondering, well, you see, I got me this girl in town...."

Anna nodded. "The schoolteacher."

Gus glanced at her in surprise. She continued peeling.

"Damn that Dutch. He probably told half the valley already."

Smiling, Anna busied herself with the potatoes. "You like this woman?"

Gus nodded.

"She like you?"

He looked at her. He turned back, spoke to the sun. "I hope so. I'd like to make her my wife."

She stopped rocking. "Gus, that's wonderful."

"I'm not so sure." The rowel of his spur spun faster.

Anna put down the potato and peeler and went over to sit next to Gus. The dog stood, climbed one step and settled his head in her lap. She stroked the bony knoll between his ears.

"If you love her, and she loves you—what's the problem?"

He looked to the horizon. "She's an educated lady, refined, like yourself. She reads books with hard covers. She listens to opera. In Italian."

She touched his hand, stopping the spinning rowel. "She reads books, she listens to music and she loves you, and you love her."

"Ain't that simple, Countess."

"Rarely is."

"I'm rough around the seams. I know which way

the wind is blowing, and I'd never kick dirt into another man's plate, but otherwise, well, what would a woman like that want with an ol' cowhand like me?"

"Have you ever asked her? I bet she'll tell you the same thing you told me—she loves you."

The cowboy shook his head. "It don't make sense."

"Some people think that's half the fun."

He sighed. "This ain't fun." He ran his hands down his chap-covered thighs. "My momma warned me if you climb into the saddle, you'd better be prepared to ride."

Anna patted his hand, the browned skin dry and lined as old leather. "There's bound to be problems sometimes, but if you love her, and she loves you, you're already ahead of the game."

"If you don't mind me asking, well, I see you and the boss together—"

"Kent and I are just friends, Gus. Good friends."

The cowboy gave her a sidelong glance. "Okay, friends it is. All I'm saying is this friendship makes the boss happy. Some days, I swear I haven't known a man happier. I look at him, and I get a twisting in my belly. I see you happy, too. Still, I'm wonderin' it must've been hard on you, coming up here with your fancy-pants background and all?"

She stood and stepped off the porch, her back turned. She folded her arms. "Sometimes I think it's the hardest thing I've ever done."

One heartbeat passed. She looked over her shoulder. "Sometimes I think it's the easiest thing I'll ever do."

She walked back to the porch. "Our situation is different from yours. You know about the accident and the amnesia. I came here to help Kent. Once he gets his memory back, things will be different. He'll be different."

She started back up the porch stairs.

"Yeah, he won't be such a lousy roper," Gus said.

"There'll be changes." She sat down in the chair and rocked back and forth. "Go ask her. Go ask your schoolteacher to marry you."

"What if she says no?"

"What if she says yes?"

The cowboy took off his hat, rubbed his hand across the raw bones of his face. "They call it 'loco' in a horse. In a man, they call it love."

He stood and shoved his hat back onto his head. The dog uncurled itself from the step, stretched once and strolled over to the man's side.

"What're you going to do? Are you going to ask her to marry you?"

He leaned down, ruffled the dog's coat. "I reckon. Damn fool that I am," he muttered as he walked away, the dog at his heels.

"Thanks, Countess." He threw the words over his shoulder.

"Let me know, Gus. I want to know."

He nodded. "You'll be the first, Countess."

She picked up a potato, the pot of peels. Gus was right. Kent was happy. The ranch was taking shape—

rotting roofs restored, fences mended, a new crop of
cows come from Colorado. She herself had scrubbed
and polished the house from top to bottom. New curtains hung on the windows. Flowers would bloom
next year at the yard's borders.

More men had been hired, more horses brought in.
Dutch complained as much as possible, but everyone
knew he was glad to have the seats at the kitchen
table full once more. Mountain John saw his son almost every other day, and Sally seemed to linger
longer each time. Now Gus had confessed his heart
belonged to another and hoped they could be together.

Without a doubt, happiness had come to the Rocking Horse Ranch. It was there in the days of dust and
sweat and caterwauling cowboys and calves scrambling after their mothers. It was in the nights of stiff
cotton sheets and fevered whispers and quick, sharp
cries sliding into laughter.

It was in moments like this when she would sit,
rocking a little rock, thinking *I am happy, I am happy.*

At times, it almost seemed real.

The front door opened behind her. Dutch walked
out onto the porch, wiping his hands on a checkered
dish towel.

"Hidin' again?" He walked over to the pot beside
the rocking chair and looked down. He looked up,
unimpressed.

"Countess, I've got me a crew of cowhands coming in, and the holes in their stomachs are gonna be
bigger than the holes in their heads."

"Then it's a good thing we'll be filling them, 'cause there's nothing worse than cranky cowboys."

"That's the idea, but between these few potatoes and the phone calls—"

"Phone calls?"

Dutch jerked his head toward the house. "That fella from L.A. whose britches are always on fire. He wants to talk to you."

She set down her bowl and peeler.

"Don't be forgettin' about these spuds," Dutch called after her.

The kitchen was rich with the smells of tonight's roast. She picked up the phone. Before she even got to the second syllable of hello, Leon said, "We're coming up there. Saturday. We'll stay overnight. Leave late Sunday. Six Japanese men plus—"

"Whoa. Wait a minute. What are you talking about?"

Leon gave an impatient breath. "I'm chartering a plane this weekend and flying the Sushima people up to the Ponderosa."

"You're serious?"

"I've no choice. The Japanese businessmen are getting impatient. I can't stall them anymore. They won't even go to the table until they see Kent. Our competitors are beginning to smell blood."

"But I thought if they saw Kent—"

"It's damned if I do, and damned if I don't. Unless my prayers are heard, and his memory comes back by Saturday. Any signs? Any more flashbacks?"

"Just those two instances I told you about."

"We've still got a few days. I'll be praying. In the meantime, all I can do is start a spin on it, tell the Japanese Kent was coming into L.A. when he thought they might enjoy doing business at his rustic hide-away."

"We can do rustic," Anna said.

"I'll tell them Kent wanted to show them the real American frontier." Leon's voice gained momentum. "How the West was won and all that crap. You can set up a hootenanny or something."

"A hootenanny?"

"You know, entertainment, a barbecue, rodeo, square dance sort of thing."

"This isn't DollyWood."

"I've got faith in you, kid. I've seen your Clean Queens act. You've got imagination."

"Don't flatter me, Leon. It makes me nervous."

"Saturday. Show time."

"What am I supposed to tell Kent? How do you expect me to explain you and a half-dozen Japanese businessmen at the Rocking Horse Ranch?"

"East meets West?"

"And I was beginning to miss you, Leon."

"I'll be there Saturday. You can hug me then."

She heard the dial tone. She glared at the receiver in her hand and called Leon a name previously reserved for Ronnie's old derby opponents. She hung up and headed back to the front porch. Dutch sat in the rocking chair, sleeping, a half-peeled potato still in one hand, the peeler in the other. Anna slid them out from between his fingers. He snored his thanks.

"Rest now, Dutch." She dragged the bag of potatoes over to the porch step and sat down. "Because this weekend, it looks like we're going to have a hootenanny."

She finished the potatoes and was putting them on the stove when Dutch came into the kitchen, his eyes still lidded with sleep. She smiled at him and, embarrassed, he waved away her comment. She started to set the table, always watching out the window, waiting for the men to come home. She saw the horses on the ridge. Dutch took the plates out of her hand.

"Go on," he said. "Go meet him."

She didn't even bother to argue. The riders were coming down the hill by the time she reached the outbuildings, so she waited there. Kent smiled when he saw her outside the stables. He reined in his horse and dismounted. The other men smiled, too, and continued on their way. She walked with Kent as he led his horse to the barn, removed its tack and, with a slap on its rump, sent it out to the pasture.

The men were heading to the bunkhouse. Kent turned to her and caught her face between his newly callused palms. His skin was warm from the sun and day's work. His breath was warmer, whispering across her cheek. She turned, not waiting, meeting his mouth, drawing his tongue inside her, and his hands slid down to where her hips dimpled. Her own hands rose to the swell of his chest, and she let him kiss her until she forgot where she was, forgot who she was, the world becoming sun-browned and smooth.

When the kiss ended, he looked down into her eyes. As if having read her thoughts, he said, "What's worrying you so, darlin', it won't wait until I've washed the day's dirt off?"

She stepped back, breaking the embrace. "Leon called today."

She saw the quick lift of his brows.

"He's coming up this weekend on Saturday and bringing some people from Sushima Components with him." She watched his eyes for recognition. What she saw was confusion.

"Why?" He began to walk toward the house.

"The Sushima people are from Japan. They're in L.A. on business."

He looked at her blankly.

"Business with Landover Tech."

He didn't say anything, kept walking.

"Leon thought they might enjoy seeing the real American West." She stumbled, and he caught her at the waist. His arm stayed there, anchoring the long length of her to his side.

"Landover Tech is my company." It wasn't a question. He stopped walking. They were both still.

"In L.A." She tried to help. "Do you remember?"

He looked past her. "There's a flash sometimes, then it's gone. It's vague, unformed, unreal."

He looked at the barns, the bunkhouse, the land rising up behind them. "This is real."

His fingers curved around her upper arms. "You're real."

Still, uncertainty colored his eyes. His hands

dropped from her arms. He began to walk, Anna beside him. "Let them come," he said.

She was silent.

"We'll brand on Saturday." He nodded. "Let them come."

He stopped in the room off the kitchen, turning the water on in the deep sink against the far wall. He stripped off his shirt and, bending his head beneath the water, wet his hair, the back of his neck. He lifted his head, shaking the damp hair off his forehead. Rivulets of water trickled between his shoulder blades, along the bars of his collarbone. He worked the soap between his hands to a thick, soft lather that squeezed between his fingers and vied with the fragrant smells coming from the kitchen. He scrubbed his skin, turning it red. Cupping his hands beneath the faucet, he splashed his face, rinsed his chest, the back of his neck, the muscles on either side of his spine rippling in rhythmic motion. Anna watched. He straightened, and she went to him with a towel, drying the hard rounds of his shoulders, the tight, proud flare of his back. Her head dipped, her tongue flickering against his moist skin. She heard his quick intake of breath, a lid dropping in the kitchen, Dutch swearing. She pulled back, drying with the towel until she saw the water like rain where his lower back met the line of his spine and hollowed. She bent down, the water soft and sweet on her tongue. He twisted, catching her by her upper arms and. pulling her to him, his chest dampening her shirtfront. He whispered, "God, woman,'' before pressing his mouth to hers and seeking the tongue that had teased his skin so artfully.

She'd heard the movements in the kitchen, knew soon the men would come from the bunkhouse. Yet she could not still her hands. They spread the width of his bare back, curled into the damp hair along his chest. She felt the press of his desire, the wide stretch of her legs until he took her by the hand and led her outside into the last warm caress of the sun. Her legs began to tremble.

''The barn,'' he whispered, and, their arms around each other again, they half ran, half stumbled like two virgin teens.

They paused in the cool darkness of the barn's entrance, their eyes adjusting. Weaving his hands through her hair, he raised her face to his, capturing her mouth once more. Her head tilted back, drinking him deeper. He ran his hands down her back, cupping them beneath her buttocks and lifting her until her trembling legs wrapped around him.

''Hurry,'' she breathed between kisses as he carried her to the small room with a cot the men used for rest when the heifers were birthing.

He set her down, ripping open her shirt, the patter of buttons against the concrete floor. He slipped his hands beneath the thin cotton, pushing the material off her shoulders and drawing it down her arms. His palms brushed back and forth against her lace-covered breasts, his fingers tracing their swell, the ache low within her. He pushed away the delicate cloth covering, exposing her, smooth and shaded in the room's half-light. His head dipped, his lips closing over first one breast, then the other, drawing her deep inside to the moist, heated circle of his mouth. She heard her breaths like puffs, like bubbles breaking at the surface.

They undressed independently, fumbling with belt buckles and zippers and boots, their breaths now coming too fast, the bang of blood at their temples. He lay down on the cot. She climbed on top, her breasts falling forward, her warm thighs on either side of him, holding him.

He reached up and pulled her down, his tongue gliding inside her as her fingers wrapped around the long silk of him and slid gently. Cupping her bottom, he brought her to him, and lifting her, hot, wet, entered her in one long, delicious move, her hands tightening on his arms, her body bowing. The taut, sure strength in his hips pressed against her, and she pressed back, his pelvis pulling her forward, pulling her back, leading her, back and forth, back and forth, the dark shades of the room seeming brighter, and the sound of laughter inside her head. Back and forth, higher, deeper until she cried out, her body seizing in long, trembling lines.

She dropped down, kissing his chest, her legs shivering against his sides. He wrapped his arms around her and she lay, felled, feeling his breaths lengthen, steady. She heard the heartbeat beneath her ear, and the moon rose and painted their flesh marble.

It wasn't until later, when they lazily rose and pulled on their clothes with drugged movements, that she remembered Leon was coming on Saturday. Leon and others into this world. Their world.

Chapter Twelve

Anna heard them first. Since sunup she'd been watching when near a window, listening when elsewhere. She woke alert, and her vigilance had heightened from there, watching, listening, waiting.

She was in the kitchen, helping with preparations for the feast following the branding, when her head came up, her body stilled. One ear cocked toward the road. The ranches were spread miles apart, and visitors were few, usually preceded by the rattle and downshift of a pickup or four-wheeler as it bounced along the rutted roads. Today's tune would be different. She listened and heard it, what she'd been waiting for since dawn: the swarming hum of foreign engines drawing near.

She wiped her hands. They held each other as she stood still a moment. Then she went outside. Two pearl-white sedans and a sports car the color of black cherries followed each other down the drive, the dust rising behind them. They stopped in the road's curve, the sun glaring off the windows, making their tinted glass even blacker.

Doors flew open. Trunk lids swung up. The first car's driver got out and walked to the back of the car, his dress suggesting someone local rather than from L.A.

Leon was the driver of the second car. Other passengers spilled out of the first two cars, all small, shiny-haired men in suits.

"Howdy, ma'am," Leon yelled in grating exaggeration. His arm swung in a wide wave. The other men turned, looked at her. She lifted her hand and walked toward the curious, black-eyed gazes. She was almost to them when the driver's door of the sports car opened. From its low-slung seat came Hilary, her hair pulled up and smooth as black ice. She wore a column of jade green that turned her eyes as cool as hidden waters. Unsmiling, she looked at Anna. Anna missed a step.

Still she called out "Hello" to the arrivals, proud of the heartiness in her voice. "Welcome to the Rocking Horse Ranch. I'm Anna," she introduced herself to the Japanese men. They nodded and smiled closemouthed.

Leon appeared from behind the slant of the trunk lid, cowboy hats in his hand. He began passing them out to the businessmen, saying, "When in Rome, gentlemen. When in Rome." The men held the hats in front of them at arm's length. They looked at the hats. They looked at each other.

"Yee-ha!" Leon put on a flat-brimmed, high-crowned hat. Too big, it slipped down his forehead. He pushed it back, smiling at the others. One by one the Japanese men put on the hats until every shiny crown was covered.

"All right." Leon rubbed his hands. "We're ready to wrestle some dogies and bust some broncs. Where's our main cowboy?"

"He's out with the other hands," Anna said. "They're rounding up the herd. We'll be branding today, and they wanted to make sure they didn't miss any stragglers."

"Branding. Rounding up the herd." Leon chanted the words, his expression turning solemn. "Gentlemen, take a good look around you. What you think you see is the American West." His arms spread wide.

"But the West is more than a stretch of land, the lowing of cattle. It's a state of mind. A philosophy of integrity, honesty and hard work. I've showed you the stats, the graphs, the sales figures. Now Kent Landover will show you the pioneer spirit that founded Landover Technology and continues to set us apart from our competitors."

Leon's voice gained power. "You'll see it, you'll experience it, you'll live it. And you'll be changed by it. Just as together, Sushima Components and Landover Technology will change the world."

His palms turned toward the sky. His eyes closed. The Japanese men looked at each other beneath their wide brims. They looked back at Leon.

"Can't you just feel it, gentlemen?" Leon breathed in, his chest ballooning. "Cowboy zen."

The men stared. Leon's hat slipped down his forehead.

He opened his eyes, pushed up his hat.

"Take it easy," Hilary said in a voice low enough for only Leon and Anna to hear. "From what I see—" her gaze circled the run-down ranch "—the one thing this place doesn't need is more manure."

"I didn't realize you were coming, Hilary," Anna said to her. She looked at Leon.

Hilary turned her cool green gaze to Anna. "I thought I should visit my fiancé. Will there be a problem?"

Anna grew conscious of the others watching. "Not at all." She turned to the Japanese men. "There are two trailers out back. They're not exactly the Hotel Bel-Air—"

"Thank God," Leon interrupted. "We're not here for creature comforts—"

"Then it looks like you came to the right place," Hilary noted in a low aside.

"We're here for the real thing, the complete enchilada." Leon's arms swept out again. "The total cowboy experience. Isn't that right, men?"

The visitors looked at him blankly from beneath the curved brims of their hats.

"Point us in the general direction. Jackson here—" with a tip of his head, Leon indicated the other driver unloading the suitcases from the trunks "—will bring the bags. Then he'll be heading out, but he'll be picking us back up tomorrow afternoon."

With Anna leading, the group started toward the house.

MORE THAN A MILE AWAY, up on top of the ridge, K.C. sat on his horse and looked down into the valley. Like Anna, he, too, had been watching, waiting. Below in the meadow's center, two men banged a bag of cow cake against the truck's tailgate. From the hills, the cattle came in long streams, the calves scrambling, the cow's low call lost before it reached the top of the ridge and K.C.

He and a few of the others had ridden up one side of the valley; the remaining men had ridden up the other side. They were looking for stragglers, making sure no cows were hiding, no calves hung up in the brush. But when K.C. reached the high point of the ridge and looked down, beyond the meadow, past the corrals and the outbuildings, he saw what he'd really been looking for all morning.

He could've said no, told them not to come. But he knew, sooner or later, they'd come anyway. They'd come like the memories, the images that had begun and couldn't be stopped.

He remembered more now. At odd moments, in eye-blink flashes, memories would superimpose themselves on his mind's eye, crowding out the now, leaving him confused. Some he didn't understand. Some he did. Not all, but enough. Enough to know that what Leon and Hilary, and even Anna, had said was true. He was that man they knew and kept talking about. A man driven, controlled, remote, impenetrable. A man who put work first and money a close second, even though there'd always been enough money. Too much money. It was the one and only security he'd ever had.

He saw this man as Leon and Hilary saw him, as the world saw him. He saw him as if seeing an old acquaintance, someone he'd known in a different time and place. Someone still not real to him. And he saw something no one else saw, not even him until now. He saw this man lonely, angry, afraid, unloved.

Until now. He thought of Anna with her sweet taste and long waist and soft shudders, and he was no longer alone. He was no longer a mere caricature of a human being. He was loved and he loved and so, was real.

He looked down into the valley. In the meadow the truck was pulling away slowly, a man throwing bits of cow cake out the back, luring the cattle to follow. Farther on, up by the house, the visitors moved single file and snakelike across the backyard toward the trailers.

He knew Anna hadn't wanted them to come. She hadn't said anything. He hadn't expected her to, but all the same, he looked into her eyes and saw the fear. The same fear he'd seen whenever he'd slipped and revealed a memory. He'd become careful. He wouldn't lose her again. He wouldn't let her leave him again.

The memories had begun to come more frequently, and he'd doubled his vigilance. He loved Anna. She loved him, K. C. Cowboy. Not some cold cardboard executive version of himself. Nobody had loved that guy.

So he said nothing about the memories. When she said Leon was coming, he pretended not to be concerned. He'd said, good, let him come, even though he knew Leon was coming here hoping to take him back, hoping to bring him home.

Let him come. Let him bring the others. It didn't matter.

With a slight press of his knees and a light tug of the reins to the left, he started his horse back down the trail. Let them come. They couldn't hurt him. He had his ranch, his men, his horses. Most of all, he had Anna. He was home.

THE JAPANESE MEN PERCHED in a neat row on the corral's top rail. They wore their cowboy hats and had changed into denim jeans, the newness of the pants revealed by their dark blue color and stiff fit. Leon wore new jeans, too, his stomach swelling above the waistband. Only Hilary, standing by the fence, wore silk the color of thick cream. Her bare arms were folded on the rail. She seemed to stand on tiptoe in her high heels. The rest of her body was touched only by air.

"I didn't know there was a woman coming," Dutch said. He'd come up behind Anna as she leaned against the back doorway, watching the bulls being cut out to a separate pen. The heat was rising. A shower not much past dawn had only been enough to wet the dust. The dampness had long since died.

"Neither did I."

"Who is she? Some hotshot lady exec?"

"She's a member of the company's board of directors."

The old man and the young woman were quiet a moment. Mountain John and the new hand shuttled the bulls. Nearby, Gus sharpened a knife.

"Kent is supposed to marry her in two weeks."

Dutch exhaled, his breath whistling low.

"Only, he forgot," she added.

The cook chuckled. "I've heard a lot of ways to beat the wedding bells, but that's an original."

"His memory will come back, and he'll remember."

"What then?"

"He'll marry her."

She felt Dutch's gaze on her. "What about you?" he finally asked.

"I'm here to help him get that memory back. Remember I told you that."

Dutch got a can of chew from his back pocket and twisted it open. "Yeah, I remember that," he said, squinting into the distance. He placed a wad of tobacco between his gum and lower lip. "I remember it, but I don't believe it."

She glanced at the man's face, loosened and lined by the years.

He looked at her. "You don't believe it, either."

She looked away, out to where a low wake of dust thickened the air. "I don't know what I believe anymore. I don't know where the reality ends and the dream begins.''

Dutch placed his hand on her shoulder. ''Hang in there, Countess. When you come to the end of the rope, tie a knot and hang on.''

She shook her head. ''I'm not a countess. I work for my mother back in L.A. She runs a cleaning service called the Clean Queens. That's me—a clean queen.''

Dutch spit a brown stream of tobacco juice. ''So?''

''Kent's not a cowboy. He's the head of Landover Tech, a computer company headquartered in L.A. Leon is his right-hand man.''

Dutch's eyebrows rose. He grinned. ''That short-plug? Levi?''

''Leon. He's been with the company since Kent started it. He's been taking care of things, covering for Kent until his memory returns.''

''What about them?'' Dutch looked at the Japanese businessmen.

''Their company is considering a partnership with Landover Tech.''

''They know about the boss's amnesia?''

Anna shook her head. ''But either they saw Kent or no deal.''

The old man threw his head back, laughter bursting out of him. One of the bulls lying in the grass, chewing, lazily turned his head and looked at the old cowboy.

Dutch shook a bandanna from his back pocket and wiped his eyes. ''They say a cow is the dumbest animal God ever created, but I don't know, you crazy city people." His head went back, and he was lost in laughter again.

"Here you all are, worried sick about the boss." Dutch chuckled, shook his head, his eyes moist with amusement. "And from where I'm standing, he's the only one with any lick of sense."

"Kent?"

"He's the one that got the hell out of there, ain't he?" Dutch began to laugh again. "He's the smartest one of the bunch."

Anna looked straight ahead, folding her arms against her chest, but she smiled.

"Listen, Countess, you said you don't know what to believe, so I'm gonna tell you. The boss don't care if you're the queen of England. He loves you. That's what you've got to believe. You don't care if he's a cowpoke or a company man. You love him, too. That's all you got to know."

Anna's smile left. She kept her gaze on the corral and the others. "It isn't that simple, Dutch." She sniffed the air. "That's not biscuits burning I smell?"

The old man spit out his chew. "Crazy city people," he muttered as he turned and went back inside the house.

Inside the fence, Mountain John gestured to the men sitting unsteadily on the top rail. "C'mon. You men want to be cowboys. It ain't gonna happen if you don't climb down off the fence."

The Japanese men looked at each other, then slid

down off the rail, their bodies seeming not to bend in their stiff jeans. Leon was the last one down.

"How 'bout you, sweetheart?" Mountain John called to Hilary. "You wannna be a cowgirl?"

Hilary stepped back farther from the fence. Her arms, still folded, drew up to her breasts. "Thank you, no."

"C'mon, darlin'," Mountain John coaxed.

Hilary took another step back. Her polite smile looked pained. She raised a manicured hand and waved no.

With a full smile, Mountain John turned to the businessmen gathered in a tight knot, glancing around at the propane-fueled fire, the sharpened knives, the syringes, the long branding irons.

"You fellas are gonna be part of the throwing crew. The boss and I will be saddling up soon and dragging the calves to the fire. Your job will be to flop the calves down so the ground crew can do their jobs. Now, if you're smart, you'll let gravity do the work. If not, you'll go pound for pound with the calf, and most times, the calf will win. Stand off to the side there, and watch the first few times."

The group shuffled gratefully back away from the red-hot fire and the branding tools.

Mountain John started to walk away, then stopped. "Any questions before we begin?" he asked the guests.

Leon stepped forward. "Which side of the cow does the brand go on?"

"We generally prefer the outside," Mountain John said, merriment crinkling the lines around his eyes.

He walked over to where his horse was grazing and swung up into the saddle, the big man's movements fluid and full of physical grace. He sat in the saddle like a king, undoing his rope, his horse moving in a slow walk. Kent, already mounted, followed, shaking out a loop.

Anna had come up to the corral and stood beside Hilary. Both women moved toward the fence, their hands taking hold of the closest rail.

The ropers eased their horses into the herd. Kent threw his loop out first, missing the calf singled out. Mountain John took his turn, the loop landing in front of the moving calf's back legs, trapping the heels. The rope was pulled tight, the other end secured around the saddle horn, and the calf was dragged, kicking and squealing, to the ground crew.

At the fire, one hand took the rope, the other the tail and wrestled the calf to the ground. Once down, a knee was braced against the calf's neck while the man's partner released the rope and stretched the hind leg out straight. After the vaccination, the men co-operated in branding and castrating the calf, then it was released to totter off in a daze toward the low call of the mothers. The entire process took less than sixty seconds.

Mountain John and Kent took turns roping and dragging the calves to the crews who, with clockwork efficiency, completed the branding process. The air thickened with dust and the smell of singed hair, scorched flesh. Anna glanced at Hilary, saw the look of horror on her face.

"Hilary, would you like to go inside? Sit down?"

The other woman turned to her, her usually placid countenance full of repulsion, her eyes as glazed as those of the bawling calves. "Go inside? I want to go home, back to L.A. and civilization. These people are barbarians. And look, look, Kent right in the middle of it all." Her throaty voice had become higher. "I dare say he enjoys it."

Anna looked at Kent as he lifted the loop, swinging it in a slow circle overhead, all the while concentrating on the area in front of the calf's hind legs. The loop snaked out, caught the calf's heels and tightened. Kent's expression stayed the same, focused, centered, intense, a quick nod of his head as the loop caught his only outward show of satisfaction.

"Roping and riding—two of a cowboy's greatest loves," Anna tried to explain.

Hilary snorted. "What's their third? Sadism?"

Mountain John called in Leon and the other businessmen, pairing them with a hand. Anna watched Leon and one of the new men wrestle a calf. A hind leg lashed out. Leon cried out, holding his shin, hopping up and down. A triumphant squeal came from another team as they threw a calf to the ground for the first time. Nearby, a Japanese man jumped back, but not before a calf squirted all over his crisp jeans and clean shoes.

"Yee-ha! You're officially cowboys now," Mountain John congratulated the men before spinning his horse around and riding back to the herd.

Anna saw the businessmen smile, including the one with the baptized boots. Even Leon, limping slightly, grinned.

Mountain John rode toward the women, drawing his horse alongside the fence. "You certain you don't want to give it a try?" he asked Hilary. "Women seem to have a natural feeling for the branding iron."

"Really?" Hilary's sultry voice only heightened the cool look crossing her features. "I would think wielding the castration knife would be our forte."

Moutain John lifted his face to the sky, releasing a rumbling laugh. "I'd have to agree it's a toss-up." He tugged at the reins, turning his horse back to the herd and the next unsuspecting calf. His face stayed lifted to the spring sunshine.

"I think he likes you," Anna said to Hilary.

"Oh, please. The man's an oaf."

"He's really very sweet. He has the cutest son—"

"They're breeding?"

The sun was high in the sky by the time the branding was finished. Anna had returned to the kitchen to help Dutch with the meal preparations. Hilary read *Vogue* on the front porch. Folding chairs had been brought out and plywood placed on two sawhorses to accommodate the overflow. Both tables were heavy with platters of glazed ham, beef, turkey, bowls piled high with potatoes, corn, peas and baskets of warm homemade bread and biscuits.

The men came in, dusty, stained, smeared with

sweat and dirt, and smiling. They needed no prompting to fill their plates and find a place to sit, the regular hands taking over the makeshift table, leaving the other for the guests. Hilary sat between Kent and Leon, looking as preserved as a pressed flower. Every now and then her eyes would dart to the raucous clamor coming from the men at the other table, before she returned her gaze to her meal cut in tiny, neat pieces. Kent hadn't been surprised to see her, nor displeased. He treated her cordially and politely, but overall was indifferent to her presence. Hilary had also turned reserved and civil, talking little, listening attentively, all the time cutting her food up into tinier and tinier pieces.

"Teamwork," Kent was saying to the businessmen.

They nodded in agreement, their mouths chewing, their hands reaching for more food. Their faces were flushed from sun and wind and hard work. Like the other men, they'd left their hats on. A few of the hats tilted rakishly.

"Each man is given a job," Kent continued, pointing with a folded piece of bread for emphasis. "He understands that job and his role in the process. He performs his particular function with the utmost efficiency, knowing his contribution is essential to the entire operation. If he falters, all falter."

The Japanese men murmured agreement.

"Each worker is a cog in the wheel, perfecting and performing his role. Each man is as important as the next, their tasks clear and defined, their service of paramount importance. The result is an optimum operation that proceeds as smooth as silk until all the work is finished.''

Kent took a big bite of the bread. ''That, gentlemen, is the beauty of branding.''

The businessmen nodded.

''But you can't forget timing, either,'' Kent went on. ''You have to know when to strike. Leave the branding iron in too long, let it get too hot, and it can do irreversible damage. On the other hand, if the time isn't right, if the iron isn't hot enough, it'll leave no impact. You've got to develop a sixth sense for the right moment, the perfect instant.''

''Yes, timing,'' one of the Japanese businessmen agreed.

''You don't want to wait too long to make your decision,'' Kent said to him. ''A cowboy who straddles the fence too long ends up with only a sore crotch.''

Hilary made a small choking noise, reached for her glass of iced tea.

''So, Mr. Landover—''

''K.C., K.C.,'' Kent insisted.

''K.C.,'' the man began again. ''These are your basic philosophies?''

''No, sir, my basic philosophy is a whole heckuva lot simpler.''

The others waited.

''Don't squat with your spurs on.''

The visitors laughed and clapped their hands. Even Hilary managed a smile.

Anna looked around the table. The guests were eating, smiling, nodding, goodwill gathering. At the other table, the hands, worn out and satisfied from a good day's work, were eating, smiling, nodding.

She looked at Kent. He caught her gaze, gave her a wink.

He'd done it again. Outsiders had come to his world, and instead of destroying it and him, he'd made them part of it. He spoke, and the Japanese men didn't see a cowboy, flushed with his first-time branding and full with a good day's work done. They saw a modern, dynamic businessman setting forth basic practices involving teamwork, international cooperation, split-second timing, experienced decision-making.

"Mr. Landover—" another visitor said.

"K.C., K.C.," Kent again insisted.

"K.C." The businessman stood, raised his glass. "You're...what they call?" He looked to his comrades, then the answer came to him and he smiled. "You're a maverick."

The other businessmen raised their glasses.

"We've enjoyed working with you today, and hope this will only be the beginning."

They applauded.

Kent raised his own glass. "Boys, whenever you're ready, the bunks have been built and the work is waiting."

Again the businessmen applauded. Leon's dirt-smeared face was radiant. Hilary, watching the discourse with keen interest, was smiling.

Kent held up halting hands. "But the work is done for today, and another will soon follow tomorrow. Now is the time to relax, to enjoy. Tonight we celebrate our newfound friendship." He looked around the table. "Right, pardners?"

The Japanese men nodded and smiled. "Pardners."

Chapter Thirteen

"Are you gonna wash those dishes or break 'em, Countess?"

The name brought her back. She'd been watching the men out the window, the hands showing off their roping skills, the visitors watching, eager to try themselves. Kent waved them over. Two of them mounted up while the others smiled encouragement and waited for their turn.

"Look at 'em," she said. "Standing out there, ankle-deep in dung, smiling as if they'd found the Elysian fields. How's he do it?"

She slammed another plate into the dish rack. Dutch picked it up, checked for chips.

"They come up here with their briefcases and double-breasted suits, and less than twelve hours later he's got them twirling a rope and yelping like they'd just won the Nevada nationals."

The glass she'd been washing chimed as it hit the rack. "Damn fools."

She heard the snicker beside her and saw Dutch's dark face wrinkle up like a raisin. "It's the chaps,

Countess," he said. His tobacco-stained teeth showed in a grin. "Makes us irresistible."

On its way to the rack, the rinsed plate caught the tip of the faucet. The pieces clanged into the sink, swirled in the running water.

Dutch took the dishrag from her hands. "Hilary's rockin' out on the porch. Maybe you could take the pot out, warm up her cup?"

Anna shook the soap bubbles off her hands and dried them. She unplugged the percolator. "Damn fools," she muttered again as she crossed the living room with the coffeepot.

Hilary looked up as the front door opened. Anna offered the pot. "Another cup?"

Hilary stopped rocking, held out her cup. "Tastes like tar."

Anna poured. "But the burn in your belly and the buzz in your brain isn't half bad."

Hilary smiled. She blew on the coffee, took a sip and began to rock again. Anna sat down on the top step. The sun was a red coal in the sky. The air was bluish above the bluffs, purple past the high peaks. The rhythmic creak of the rocker steadied her thoughts. Still her anger didn't ease.

"That was quite a show," Hilary said.

Anna turned, looked up at the woman.

Hilary rocked with an even pace. "Either he's the luckiest bastard that ever lived or the cleverest. I hadn't decided which yet."

. Anna knew she was talking about supper and the Japanese men's ready embrace of Kent's "cowboyin''' talk as a metaphor for his business philosophy.

Hilary took another sip of coffee. "Of course, Leon did have them all pumped and primed with his snake oil show, selling them the metaphysics of the Wild West, making Kent out like Gandhi in a cowboy hat."

"It's not an act with Kent. He believes he's K.C." Anna tried to explain to Hilary, to herself. "His belief is so powerful, so absolute, it spreads to those around him and becomes reality. That's what you saw tonight at supper. Those businessmen are out back right now, ready to run off and join the rodeo."

"What about you?" Hilary rocked, watched Anna.

"Me?"

"You've been up here over a week with him, but you seem immune to all this nonsense. Maybe *cowboyin'* is only carried by the Y chromosome?"

Anna turned away. She might know this world wasn't real, but that didn't mean she didn't believe in it. She had believed in it. She'd believed in him, in her, in their love. She was worse than the smiling men out back in their stiff-legged jeans. Her anger turned inward.

"I'm not immune."

Hilary made no response, rocked.

"Do you love him, Hilary?" she had to ask.

The creak of the rocker stopped. "What do you mean?"

She looked up at the elegant woman. "You're going to marry him. Do you love him?"

Hilary's cheeks hollowed. "Love is for children

and fools. Kent and I understand each other. We grew up in the same circles. We have similar backgrounds and similar goals. We both know what we want and how to get it and we aren't going to apologize for taking it.''

Anna turned away again.

''You've fallen in love with him, haven't you?''

She suffered Hilary's low, amused laugh.

''You've lived with him for about a week, slept with him, what? Four, five, six times? Now you're in love.''

Anna said nothing. She couldn't deny her feelings, nor could she defend them. Both women knew she'd fallen in love with an illusion.

Hilary got up, dumped the remains of her coffee over the rail. ''We should've seen this coming.'' She sat down beside Anna, smoothed the silk creases of her pants. ''It was like sending a lamb to the lion.''

Anna continued to look straight ahead.

''Oh, honey.'' Hilary lifted her hand, hesitated, then patted Anna clumsily on the shoulder. ''What were you thinking? You know it's only a matter of time until Kent's memory returns, and everything goes back to the way it was before. You're a lovely girl.'' Hilary offered an awkward pat once more. ''But did you really believe once Kent's memory came back, the relationship would continue?''

Anna looked straight ahead. She'd been a fool.

''It's okay, darling.'' The amusement in Hilary's voice had been replaced by pity. ''You got caught up in it. That's all. Just like the boys out back, you believed all this.''

Anna sat silent. She heard the night insects readying their song. She saw the land rolling away from her, felt the give of the wood beneath her feet. The sting of dust was in the air. It was the most beautiful place on earth.

''I believed,'' she said.

Hilary stood up, stepped down off the porch. ''I knew this was a bad idea. *Challenge the illusion*,'' her voice mocked. ''It had the AMA seal of approval. Send him off to his ranch. Let him ride into the sunset. He'll be safe, away from the city, and back to his senses before you can sing 'Whoopee Ti Yi Yo.'''

Hilary looked around her. ''*Challenge the illusion*, my foot. He's got his horse, his stinking cows, the gang that couldn't shoot straight, a cook that looks like he's spent one too many days on the wagon trail.'' She paused, looked at Anna. ''And he's got you.''

She touched her hair, her hands plumping the ends curved under. ''This isn't challenging the illusion. This is catering to the illusion.''

Anna knew she was right.

''Leon and his brainstorms. If he'd just listened to me, the petition for temporary guardianship would already have been filed.''

''Temporary guardianship?''

''Of course, it was too big a risk before with the Sushima people due in the following week, but we don't seem to have that problem any longer. On the contrary, a little dust, a lot of manure, some calf mutilation and gibberish about the 'cowboy way,' and these men are ready to hitch their wagon to Landover Tech. All's well that ends well, except I've got over six hundred guests expecting to toast the union of Landover and Fairchild next weekend, and the groom is up here, playing 'King of the Cowboys.'"

"Temporary guardianship?" Anna asked again.

"Look around you. Look at this place. The man obviously isn't competent to control his own affairs anymore."

"You're serious."

Hilary looked down at her. "I would be doing you a favor. The longer this goes on, the more painful it'll be when it ends. And it will end, Anna. You know that as well as I do."

She had no argument.

Hilary sat back down. "The quicker we can shut down this fiasco, the better. Too much money has already been squandered on this place."

"What?"

Hilary looked at her. "Buying this ranch is a prime example of Kent's irrational state of mind. Ranches are losing investments. This one looks like it lost the battle a long time ago. We'll be lucky if we can break even by selling the land—"

"What about the men?"

Hilary stared at her. "God, you're a romantic."

Anna knew it wasn't a compliment.

"I may sound harsh, but, believe me, I've been patient. I sat back quietly and let Leon make the decisions. I came up here hoping to find some progress, some sign.''

"But Leon must have told you Kent had a few instances when he seemed to remember?''

"Too little, too late.''

"Don't do it, Hilary.''

"Things can't continue this way. Time is running out. Somebody's got to do something, and there doesn't seem to be any other solution.''

Anna looked out at this place she'd come to love. She thought of the man she'd always loved. "There may be one other solution.''

"What?'' the other woman demanded.

She couldn't be angry with Hilary. Hilary spoke only the truth. She was angry only with herself.

She'd known from the beginning it would end. She'd known it would break her heart. And still she'd loved.

She sat on the step, feeling tall and thin and un-gainly, knowing she would have felt that way even if Hilary hadn't been beside her. She sat on the step and let the pain come.

"I'll leave,'' she said.

THE DAY HAD BEEN LONG, the hour seeming later than it was. The men had gone to the bunkhouse for shots of whiskey and a few hands of poker. Hilary had re-tired to the spare bedroom Anna had set up for her. In his ongoing enthusiasm for the "cowboy experi-ence,'' Leon had refused Kent's offer of his bedroom, insisting he would sleep in the bunkhouse. It wasn't until after Kent told him the combination of poker and whiskey was one of the top ten causes of death among cowboys that Leon decided to accept Kent's offer.

Anna was waiting outside for Kent as he came up from the barns to get his bedroll and take it down to the bunkhouse.

He smiled when he saw her standing there. He came to her, and, before she could get a word out, he pulled her into his arms, pressing his mouth to hers. He lightly bit her bottom lip. Her lips parted. His tongue moved inside, and he took her body tighter to him, his textures wet and dry, desert and sea, his hollows hard, his breath soft.

He smelled of the wind. So familiar was his touch, his taste, his hand moving, molding to her breast, she forgot what was to come and thought only of now, the surge of promise between her legs. Her hands curved to the strength of his back, her own body arching and the night falling. Finally she broke away, stepping back from the embrace. She looked at him. His fingers ringed her wrist as if she might run. She knew then the pain and fear were in her eyes.

"What is it?" he said. His gaze would not leave hers.

She wouldn't cry. She didn't have to. She'd already given herself away. She looked past him.

"What's wrong?" His fingers were too tight on her arm.

"You're hurting me."

He dropped her wrist, the stricken expression on his face revealing he hadn't realized.

She looked into his eyes, placed her hand to his cheek. How could she go?

She took her hand away. She saw that the fear in her eyes had caught in his.

"Tell me," he said, the demand in his voice.

Only two words had to be said. Still her throat closed, and her mind searched like a mouse in a maze for another solution. There was none. Despite the doctors' recommendations and Leon's predictions, the situation hadn't gotten better. On the contrary, it'd become worse. The fantasy had become reality not only for Kent, but for those around him. The others had come, and she'd seen them too easily persuaded to pretend. She'd been just as willing to believe. Believe in Kent's world, now her world, a world not real.

This world, their world, had been created once before, then destroyed; now, through dreams and desire, Kent and she had created it again. As long as they were together, it would continue. Only if she left would the fantasy be over. Reality regained. Reason and Kent's memory restored.

She swallowed the thickness in her throat. She wasn't so naive as to think her own heart would survive. It had long ago succumbed. She thought of the skin near his shoulder blade, how it tasted warm, how his head would drop when her lips touched him there. God, she would miss him.

She stood before him, her hands behind her back, holding on to each other, tendon and bone.

"I'm leaving."

For a moment there was nothing. Then she watched his body stiffen, bone by bone. Her own hands twisted.

"Leaving—?" He drew the word out, drawling the sounds, his neck thrust forward. His mouth remained open as if more words were to come, but there was only breath, the rise and fall of his chest. She watched his breastbone lift, lower.

"I came here to…" she began.

His shoulders rose with a breath. He was mere air. No more. She couldn't speak any longer.

"You came here to what? To see?" He filled in the blank. "To see if you could lie with a man and forget his hands were rough, and his speech simple, and his skin smelled of sweat?"

She lifted her face. "No."

"You dressed in faded clothes, you slept in a monk's room, you chapped your hands cleaning, strained your eyes sewing. You came here to see. To see what life would be like with me."

"No."

"I'm a cowboy, Anna."

"No." She fisted her hands, brought them to her temples.

"You're a countess. I've always understood that. We can't change what we are."

"You don't understand."

"I worried, too. I worried when you told me people

were coming from L.A., people who would remind you of the life you left. I worried the differences would always be too great, that the longing, one day, could no longer be ignored. I knew from the beginning I had no right to love you.''

She could only plead, ''You've got it inside out. You were the one born rich, raised in wealth, schooled in the best schools, destined to be successful and accomplished. You're the head of your own company, a businessman envied by your competitors. My mother worked for your family. She waxed your mother's floors, took a toothbrush and scrubbed clean the bathtub grout, ironed her silk panties. I'm her daughter. No more. Yes, your world and my world are day and night, but you're the one from the privileged class. Your kind don't love women like me. They hire them.''

''What are you talking about? Look at me. Look at me.''

''No, you look at me. Look at me. See me. Remember me.''

They stood, their gazes weaving into one.

''You're all I remember, Anna.''

She had to turn away then, turn to the web of the night, seeking its black strength.

''I came here to help you get your memory back. The doctors and Leon said there was a good chance your memory would return once your fantasy was challenged. Only, the fantasy wasn't challenged. It became real. By coming here, I didn't help you. I hurt you. I don't know if your memory will come back if

I leave, but I do know that as long as I'm here, you won't get better. I know you don't understand now, but you will once your memory comes back. You'll understand none of this was real.''

He grasped her arm and pulled her tight against him. "This isn't real?''

She felt the heat of his flesh, saw the bright pain in his eyes.

He captured her hand, forced its palm to his chest. "Feel me. This isn't real?''

His fingers pressed into the tender underside of her arm. "Tell me you don't love me.''

She looked away from the fury twisting his features.

"Say it.'' His breath was hot across her cheek. "Say it.''

She twisted her arm. "Let me go.'' He held her fast while she wriggled like a tethered animal.

"Say it.''

She twisted her face to his. Their mouths almost met. "I won't,'' she cried out. "I won't.'' Her voice broke. "At least give me that.''

His hand dropped away from her, the freedom so sudden, she stumbled backward. They faced each other, their breaths coming in great drafts. She rubbed the bruised flesh of her arm.

"I'm leaving with the others tomorrow. Your memory will come back, and everything will make sense once more. You'll go on with your life.''

The fury in his eyes flared, and she stepped back, but he made no movement toward her. The blaze in his eyes burned itself out as quickly as it had ignited. His eyes turned the color of ashes.

"You're my life," he said. "And this is real. You and me. It's the only thing that is real."

He turned and left her. She watched him walk into the night and the dreams that lay waiting. She stood there a long time, long after his figure blended with the darkness. The dark air shifted, seeped inside her. Her heart became the night, still, shuttered, full of secrets. The night that could be friend or foe. Still she stood there, in her enemy's arms, everything else shadows. She didn't move, and dissolving into darkness and pain, was no more. There was only the night.

Her love had walked to the barn, to the cramped shelter of the tack room. He turned on a small lamp set near the bench, and selected a bridle from the many hanging. He got the polish and a rag and went to work. There would be no sleep tonight. He felt the cool silver of the bit in his fingers, the leather straps warm as they lay across his legs. He spread the polish, its scent releasing. He rubbed with strong, even rhythm. Back and forth, back and forth. He heard the shuffle of the animals, the crickets' evening call, the sigh of the night. He let his rigid shoulders sag. He slid to his knees, his body doubling up, the cool silver clenched in his hand.

Chapter Fourteen

There was little to pack. She zippered the silver tote. She had told herself she wouldn't stay long. She'd been right. She put the tote and the duffel by the door. She looked in the drawers and closet to make sure they were empty. She straightened the pillow on the bed and smoothed the bedcovers where she'd lain awake all night, her hands lingering on the old quilt a moment longer than needed.

Half the guests had gone on a trail ride. The other half were touring the land by truck. She'd already talked to Leon and Hilary, taking them aside before they headed out with the others. Leon had protested when she told them she'd be leaving, but his arguments couldn't sway her. Aware of Anna's intentions since yesterday, Hilary only nodded.

Leon and the other businessmen were leaving at four that afternoon to make their charter. Hilary and Anna would leave then, too, but because Hilary preferred her feet on the ground as much as possible, the two women would drive back to L.A.

Anna took a final look around the small bedroom—

the worn furniture, the wood floors, scratched and dull but warm to bare soles in the morning. She hadn't left anything behind. She picked up her bags, carried them downstairs to the front porch, then went into the kitchen to help Dutch. She talked little, only to ask what should be done next or comment on the possibility of rain later in the day.

Dutch was unusually quiet also, his gaze darting every now and then to her. She'd also told him earlier that she had to go. He'd pushed his hat back off his brow and scratched his forehead, looking at her. Finally he'd said, "No cappuccino machines, huh?"

Smiling, she'd put an arm around his shoulders and kissed his weathered cheek. "You take good care of these cowboys," she'd whispered.

"Somebody's gotta," he'd said in his always gruff voice. "Being their brain cavities wouldn't hold 'nough water for a cactus plant."

She didn't see Kent until midafternoon. It was the first she'd seen him since last night. She'd skipped breakfast to avoid him, but Dutch had let her know Kent hadn't shown up either for eggs and sourdough biscuits.

Outside now, Dutch was heating oil in a cast-iron kettle suspended by a chain over a log fire. She was in the kitchen, slicing the bread and counting off in her head how many would be sitting down. She glanced out the window, and there he was, closing the fence gate. She couldn't take her eyes off him.

He headed into the barn, then came back out with two halters—one braided rope, the other leather. He brought them over to two of the Japanese businessmen standing nearby. Gone was the loose-jointed stance, the easy-coming smile. He pointed to something on one halter, then compared the other. Even at a distance, Anna could see the tight draw of his mouth. She looked away. Out by the kettle, Dutch had pierced four steaks on each tine of a pitchfork and was lowering them into the hot oil. The meal would be ready soon. She turned to set the table.

THE KITCHEN WAS as crowded as the night before; those gathered around the table as talkative except for two. When he'd first come in, she'd turned, and seeing it was him, her hand had risen and touched her throat. He had nodded to her, his expression arranged in careful lines. Then he'd looked at her no more. He went to his place at the table and sat, his movements contained, his rare comment polite. When she rose to get the other basket of bread warming on the oven, he'd drawn his body forward as she'd passed.

They were sitting on the front porch, finishing cake and coffee, when the hired driver pulled up and parked the cream sedan next to the others waiting to leave. Before dessert was served, the hands had brought up the guests' bags. They'd lingered, wanting to say goodbye.

Anna hugged them one by one. She knew they would talk of her later, speculate on her sudden leave-taking, but for now, each one just squeezed her hard. She almost got away with no more than a forced smile until Gus embraced her and whispered in her ear, "She said yes, Countess." She pressed her face to his

shoulder and held on to him tight until she was sure
no more tears would come.

Kent had walked his guests to their cars, had
shaken their hands, wished them a safe trip. He'd
walked back, standing apart from the others, not
seeming to look at anything in particular. Anna
walked toward him, remembering the first time they'd
come here, the first night they'd lain together, remembering...

He wouldn't look at her. She could only look at
him.

"Goodbye." She didn't touch him. She didn't say
anything else. She didn't know what to say. She loved
him. His gaze stayed riveted at a point past her.

She began to turn when he caught her waist,
brought her to him. "Stay," he whispered hoarsely.
His mouth came down on hers, his breath life itself.
Taken by surprise, her strength folded, and she felt
herself sinking into him, felt the chafe of his unshaven
skin, her lips clinging to his in anguish and ecstasy,
and the easy roll of tears beginning again.

Then he pushed her away, his hands holding her at
arm's length, the air drying the tears on her skin.
"Go," he ordered. She saw a stranger on her last
look, the anger and pain having forged a new face.

The others looked away as she walked to the humming sports car, sleek and wine colored. She got into
the seat, its too-low curves stretching her body long
like a tender lover. She still tasted Kent, raw and tor-
turous, on her lips.

With a sidelong glance, Hilary questioned her, her
manicured hand clutching the stick shift.

"Go," Anna ordered.

KENT KNEW WHO HE WAS. He woke as if he hadn't slept at all and remembered everything. He eased himself up from the hard ground that'd been his bed. The day was breaking around him. He hadn't thought he could sleep, and now, remembering images more real than dreams, wondered if he had.

He'd seen himself so young, running through the kitchen, the cook scolding, and he, ignoring him and running, as if winged, out the back door. He'd run across the squares of yard, and life was everywhere— in the budding flowers, the stubborn weeds, the heated air, the burn in his chest.

"Anna," he'd called as he ran, even though he knew she couldn't hear him. Still, he called, "Anna," the name lifting and offered to the spring sounds.

Finally he'd reached the tiny house with the trim the color of melted sunlight and the gaily striped curtains. He'd pounded on the door. He had news to share and secrets to tell and the need to be near her. He'd called out, "Anna," in his rich, urgent voice.

He'd waited several seconds, shifting from foot to foot, then his fist banged again. He'd looked into the windows, at first seeing only his own reflection, the narrow shoulders, the thin neck, his ears too big beneath the black cowboy hat edged in white and decorated with cheap metal. His eyes adjusted, his own image fading, revealing a house, still and empty. The sofa and the one wing chair had been stripped of the lacy doilies Anna's mother crocheted and smoothed each day across their arms and backs. The small throw pillows he and Anna had helped stuff were gone. There'd been two plastic-framed pictures on the end table. One was of a handsome young man in a T-shirt smiling and squinting into the camera. The other was of the same man, this time looking down, his large hands cradling a blanketed bundle. Now the end table was bare. The narrow closet near the front door was open and empty. The brim of Kent's hat had bent as he'd pressed his face against the glass.

He'd stepped back, his own reflection returning. Anna was gone. He'd felt the prickly pressure at the back of his eyes. She'd left him—just like the others did. Why? He'd swallowed the strangling sensation creeping up his throat. He had to be careful not to let anyone see him cry. He'd go to the barn, press his face to Lightning's coarse mane. Only then would he cry, his sobs muffled by the flat stretch of the horse's neck, his sadness soothed by the animal's warmth. Then he'd remembered. Lightning was gone.

Anna was gone.

He'd stepped back from the window, and he, too, was gone. He'd walked away from the empty house. On the ground lay the black cowboy hat. Beside it lay the thick gold chain studded with red stones he'd brought for the dress-up box.

The streaked morning sky became blue. Kent sat, not feeling the first warmth of the sun, and remembered. For the first time, he knew who he was. Where he began, where he ended. Some knew him as a shrewd and practical businessman; others knew him as a man of the land. But he alone knew who he was. He was a man who loved Anna.

Now Anna was gone.

And he was no more.

ON HER HANDS AND KNEES, Anna squeezed farther into the space between the wall and the toilet; her scrub brush aimed at the narrow stretch of floor behind the bowl's base.

As she inched her way forward, her gaze focused on the discolored tile, she could hear her mother.

You don't have to clean anymore.

It had been bad enough in the office, suffering Ronnie's sorrowful looks. She didn't need her mother's gentle but firm voice following her, too.

There's enough girls to handle the jobs and a ready list of replacements.

But two days sitting behind a desk had been two days too many. Too many lulls and her body too still. Too much time to think, to remember. Too many sympathetic glances from Ronnie; too many overly cheerful choruses of "Oklahoma" from her mother. And so Anna cleaned, scrubbing the surfaces long after they shone, scouring the finishes until damage threatened.

"Gotcha, sucker," she said, applying fresh force to the stain on the floor. She didn't know what it was, and she didn't want to find out. She thought as little as possible these days. If she didn't think, she didn't remember. If she didn't remember, she was okay. She was okay.

She heard footsteps, heard the door swing open, but wedged between the wall and the toilet, she couldn't turn to see who it was. "Mora?" she said.

She backed out on her hands and knees from behind the toilet bowl, her backside greeting whoever had come into the bathroom. It was in this inelegant position that she saw the cowboy boots. She froze, her rump still pointing high and hello. She was about to scurry back into the thin space like a trapped rat when she heard "Anna?"

Damn, he'd recognized her smile.

She sat back on her haunches, felt the flush on her face, waved a weak hello with her scrub brush. Kent stood over her, seeming larger than life in the tiny room. He offered his hand.

She stared at it, remembering his touch, the curl of his fingers along her rib cage. She saw that two blisters on the pads of his palm had turned into thick skin. She peeled off the yellow rubber glove she wore, gave him her hand if only to show she could touch him and not shatter.

She was wrong. His flesh met hers, and the equilibrium she'd proudly maintained this past week crumbled. She pulled her hand away, resisted the urge to step back to the cool support of the wall.

She looked at him. If he said "Howdy" she'd scream. But, besides the boots, he was Botany 500: tailored chalk-striped suit, Italian silk tie, a fine-grained cotton shirt. She stared at this mix of cowboy and CEO.

"Hello," he said.

"Hello," she answered.

There was a pause as if they were two strangers.

"Your mother told me where you were. The night watchman recognized me, let me in."

Anna nodded, waited for him to say something more. What was he doing here?

He looked around the executive washroom. "Nice sink."

Nice sink? "It's marble."

He shoved his hands into his front pants pockets and looked at her. She looked away, brushed off some of the powdered cleanser sprinkled across her Clean Queens T-shirt.

He wasn't K. C. Cowboy, nor was he the controlled, cool-headed Kent Landover. Who was he now?

"I saw your picture in the paper with the Sushima executives. Deal of the century," she said. "Congratulations."

"Thank you." He jingled the keys in his pocket.

"You must be very happy. Leon must be unbearable."

He smiled. All her defenses fell away. Would she ever stop loving him?

She knew she couldn't take much more. "What are you doing here?"

He cleared his throat. "There's a wedding."

She stared at him. "Yes, I know."

"You're invited."

At first she didn't think she'd be able to reply. She stood there, staring, shaken. His expression was similarly uncertain.

Finally she was able to form a coherent response. "No."

His forehead wrinkled into deep lines. He moistened his lips. "I know it's an imposition—"

Imposition?

"But it would mean a lot if you could come."

"No." It was the best she could do at this point.

"The others will be there."

Obviously she had to do better than "no." She took a breath. "I'm sure it'll be the social event of the season."

One corner of his mouth tipped. "Probably." The keys jangled. "We could go together."

She stared at him. Disbelief glazed her features. "I don't think the bride would appreciate that."

His brow tightened further. "Why?"

"Why?" she erupted. "I don't think bringing a date to your own wedding would fly—not even in California."

"My wedding?" His confusion continued. "I'm not getting married."

She stared at him with the same disbelief. "Does Hilary know?"

He let out a laugh. Still the tenseness in the air remained.

"She drove a hard bargain—born negotiator—but we were able to come to terms. I gave her what she really wanted all along—one-third of my stock and a major role in the company. She's the new head of product progress."

She listened to his soft laugh.

"She stuck me with two silver birch arbors, a bill for a Vera Wang original and enough foie gras and lobster tortellini to feed a small, underdeveloped country."

Anna looked at the man before her. When he

laughed, she saw K. C. Cowboy. When he stood silent, his expression concentrated, she saw Kent Coleman Landover, CEO. When he looked at her now, the laughter still in his face, the tenderness in his eyes, she saw a man. Only a man.

"It's Gus who's getting married. He said you knew."

"I did. I do, but I thought, well, I knew you and Hilary—"

"No, I'm not marrying Hilary. Not now," he said as he looked into her eyes. "Not now." His voice went low, and his body seemed to relax, his shoulders curving toward her.

Then he straightened as if catching himself. "Could you see her on the ranch? She'd bring her Wolfgang Puck cookbook into Dutch's kitchen, and it'd be worse than the Battle of Little Big Horn."

"You kept the ranch?"

"Kept it? I'm going to run it."

"What about Landover Tech?"

"I'll come in a couple days a month. The rest I can oversee from the Rocking Horse. That's the beauty of computers. Between Leon and Hilary, I won't even be missed."

She could only stare at him as she had since she'd first looked up and seen him above her. She knew this man, yet she didn't. "The amnesia—?"

"All gone. My memory came back completely. I remember everything, Anna. Everything before the accident. Everything after." The eyes that looked at her were too blue. "Most of all, I remember how happy

I was at the ranch. I'd never been that happy before…except once.''

If only she could look away, not be caught in the
spell again.

"Come with me, Anna."

"To the wedding?"

"For a start."

No, she thought, not another start to something that
wouldn't last. Her heart couldn't take it again.

"No," she said out loud to his offer, to her love.

His mouth opened.

"No," she said again before his words could come
and weave their magic, before his hand reached for
hers.

"Thank you anyway." She pulled the rubber glove
back on. "I have to finish here."

His mouth was still open. For a moment she was
afraid he'd try to persuade her. For a moment she
feared he wouldn't. She didn't know which she
wanted more. She dropped the brush into a plastic
bucket, picked up its handle.

"I see," he said. Still he made no movement. She
feared she would weaken.

Then he took his hands out of his pockets, drew
himself up. "I'll let you get back to work."

Her smile was false; her voice was false. "It was
nice seeing you."

He didn't have to look at her one more time like
that, but he did. "Goodbye, Anna."

He was gone.

"Goodbye," she whispered. She picked up the pail
and walked out of the room scrubbed clean.

HE CURSED AT HIMSELF every step, using every pro-
fanity he knew and a few he'd just learned from
Dutch and the boys. What was that? he berated himself. One *no,* and he'd folded like a house of cards?
Okay, she hadn't wanted to go to the wedding. What
about coffee? He could've asked her out for coffee
when she finished the job. He could've told her he
knew she hadn't gotten her quota of cappuccino while
up at the ranch.

He should've said anything. Instead, he'd walked
out. K.C. wouldn't have walked out. K.C. would have
handed her his heart on a platter. But he wasn't K.C.
anymore. The old Kent wouldn't even have seen her
again, suppressing any feelings beneath a smooth
shell. But he wasn't the old Kent, either. He was a
man in love with Anna.

And he didn't want her to just have coffee with
him. He didn't want her to only go to the wedding
with him. He wanted her with him. All the time. Forever. He needed her.

That's what he should have told her, he thought as
he jammed his keys into the car door. That's what
K.C. would've told her. Again and again until she
drew near, and he gathered her to his heart.

He missed K.C. He missed Anna.

He unlocked his car. He wasn't a child any longer,
the voice in his head told him. A child who felt pow-
erless to prevent love from leaving his life. He was a
man now.

He pulled the keys out. Turned around.

She wasn't in the bathroom off the large office anymore. He walked down the hall. Farther up on the

left, a door was propped open, a light on. He stopped in the doorway. It was a ladies' rest room. At first he didn't see anyone and was about to turn around when he spied the white running shoes beneath the middle stall's door.

He stepped into the room smelling of lavender.

"I'm cleaning in here," he heard muffled from inside the stall.

"I know, I know you have cleaning to do," he said. He took a breath. "But I've got something to say, and I'm afraid if I don't say it now, I never will. I've already waited too long, wasted so much time."

He didn't risk waiting for her permission. "I'm not K.C., but sometimes I wish I was again. He wasn't afraid. He wasn't afraid of anything—not you, not love."

"But—" he heard from inside the stall.

"Please let me finish. I blamed everyone else—my father, my mother, even you for leaving me, but now I've learned I was to blame, too. The jewelry, the amnesia, my fear to open my heart to another, to express the emotions inside me. I was afraid of being vulnerable. I made the choice to hide behind work, success, power, money. Love, I decided, I would leave to others. I was afraid.

"I grew up, and I succeeded. I had everything— wealth, intelligence, position. Everything except happiness. And so I had nothing. Still, I couldn't face my fear—until one day I saw you again and remembered. Remembered what happiness was like. Yet even then, my fear was so great, I couldn't take the risk. Enter K. C. Cowboy.

"K. C. Cowboy is gone now, and I'm still afraid. But I'm more afraid of losing you. We've lost so many years, so much time. I don't want to lose a second more."

Before he took another breath, he said, "I love you, Anna. I love you, and I want you to be my wife."

He heard the catch of breath behind him and turned. Anna stood in the doorway, a roll of paper towels in each hand.

He looked at her, then back to the stall door, running his hand through his hair. "I thought..."

"It doesn't matter."

He rubbed his forehead. "Tell me you heard everything I said, because I don't think I can go through it again."

The stall door swung open, and a small, dark-complected woman holding a toilet bowl brush stepped out. "Anna, he says—"

Anna waved her hand. "I heard, Mora." Her gaze stayed on Kent. "I heard."

"Yeah?" The woman looked at Kent, nodded her head in approval. "Whaddya say? 'Cause if you don't want him, I've got a sister..."

Anna looked into Kent's eyes, saw his fear, his courage, his need. Above all, she saw his love.

"I want him."

And she was in his arms, his mouth to hers.

Mora picked up the paper towel packages rolling across the floor and, smiling, slipped past the lovers and out of the room.

Kent's mouth moved away only to kiss her cheek, her forehead, the tip of her nose. Her hands moved up and down the length of his arms, tightened on the solidness of his shoulders.

"Anna," he said in a voice suddenly so serious, she felt her own eyes widen with question.

"I'm not a cowboy," he confessed.

Her laughter echoed in the tiled room. She looked at her love with smiling eyes. "I'm not a countess."

He took both her hands as if determined they would never slip from his reach again. "After these last few weeks, I'm not sure who I am. Except when I look into your eyes. Then I exist."

His mouth touched hers, and Anna herself was born in that moment.

A moment when two adults finally understood what two children had always known so many years ago. A moment when two hearts that had been silent all those many years began to beat again.

presents

CAUGHT WITH A COWBOY

A new duo by
Charlotte Maclay

Two sisters looking for love
in all the wrong places...
Their search ultimately leads them
to the wrong bed, where they
each unexpectedly find
the cowboy of their dreams!

THE RIGHT COWBOY'S BED (#821)
ON SALE APRIL 2000

IN A COWBOY'S EMBRACE (#825)
ON SALE MAY 2000

Available at your favorite retail outlet.

Makes any time special ™

Mother's Day is Around the Corner...
Give the gift that celebrates Life and Love!

Show Mom you care by presenting her with a one-year subscription to:

HARLEQUIN WORLD'S BEST

Romances

For only **$4.96**—
That's **75% off the cover price.**

This easy-to-carry, compact magazine delivers 4 exciting romance stories by some of the very best romance authors in the world.

Plus each issue features personal moments with the authors, author biographies, a crossword puzzle and more...

A one-year subscription includes 6 issues full of love, romance and excitement to warm the heart.

To send a gift subscription, write the recipient's name and address on the coupon below, enclose a check for $4.96 and mail it today. In a few weeks, we will send you an acknowledgment letter and a special postcard so you can notify this lucky person that a fabulous gift is on the way!

A special feeling,
   A special secret...
      No one blossoms more beautifully
         than a woman who's

With Child...

And the right man for her
will cherish the gift of love she brings.

**Join American Romance and four
wonderful authors for the event of a lifetime!**

THAT'S *OUR* BABY!
Pamela Browning
March 2000

HAVING THE BILLIONAIRE'S BABY
Ann Haven
April 2000

THAT NIGHT WE MADE BABY
Mary Anne Wilson
May 2000

MY LITTLE ONE
Linda Randall Wisdom
June 2000

Available at your favorite retail outlet.

HARLEQUIN®
Makes any time special ™

Visit us at www.romance.net

HARWC

COMING NEXT MONTH

#821 THE RIGHT COWBOY'S BED by Charlotte Maclay
Caught with a Cowboy!
Though Ella Papadakis found herself in the wrong bed, she'd found the
right cowboy. Now, if she could just convince Bryant Swain that they were
meant to be together. With their baby on the way, Bryant agreed to a
marriage in name only, but Ella wasn't going to rest until she lassoed the
cowboy into admitting he wanted happily-ever-after, too!

#822 LAST-MINUTE MARRIAGE by Karen Toller Whittenburg
Brad Keneally's overprotective ways drove Zoë Martin crazy. But when
Brad suddenly asked Zoë to pretend to be his wife for two weeks, she said
yes! Being close to Brad forced Zoë to admit the truth—she'd secretly
loved him for years. Was it too late to turn a last-minute marriage into the
love of a lifetime?

#823 A PRECIOUS INHERITANCE by Emily Dalton
An unexpected tragedy had landed three little girls in Spencer Jones's
custody—and Alexandra Ethington into his life. As a small-town doctor,
Spencer valued the importance of family and he was ready to make
Alexandra his wife...until he learned she was the girls' aunt. Did
Alexandra just want custody, or was she genuinely interested in Spencer?

#824 HAVING THE BILLIONAIRE'S BABY by Anne Haven
With Child...
He was rich, he was sexy...and he was going to be a daddy! When
Serena Jones realized that her brief affair with business tycoon
Graham Richards had resulted in a bundle of joy, her protective
instincts told her to keep the child a secret. After all, the last thing
Graham wanted was a family, right?

Visit us at www.romance.net